CW00345464

PERFECT

JoAnne Stefanizzi

The characters and events portrayed in this book are fictional and any similarity to actual persons, living or dead, is entirely coincidental and not intended by the author

Copyright 2020
JoAnne Stefanizzi

All rights reserved

No part of this book may be reproduced, or stored in a retrieval system, or transmitted in any form or by any means, electronic, mechanical, photocopying, recording or otherwise, without express written permission of the publisher, except by reviewers, who may quote brief passages in a review

ISBN: 9798622214028

Dedicated to my very supportive and loving husband Joe, my two wonderful sons, Joe and Dan and to the writing community at ABCTALES.com for all the kind support and helpful critiques they've offered me along my writer's journey.

CHAPTER 1

The bright lights of the hospital's newborn room were blinding and the babies' cries were deafening. Angelica wished a nurse would come to quiet their fears. She wished someone could quiet hers. She was not ready to concede, not ready to let go. Certainly not ready to begin this next lifetime.

The harsh sentence of the Council Most High was a decision she did not agree with and one she would fight for as long as she could but her eye lids were becoming heavy, and it was getting harder to fight off the desire to close them.

Determination was all she had; there was no other way to avoid the inevitable.

Angelica stared at the stark, white lights of the nursery wanting to change the decision they'd made for her and the words Orion had spoken replayed in her thoughts.

"Angelica, we have decided you shall have the privilege of a new life. Have you any questions before it is set?"

Did she have questions? Yes, she had questions and an opinion that differed radically, but finding her voice to speak them was nearly impossible. She was petrified of this decision.

"Then it is set-"

"Wait," she squeaked, her voice barely audible as all the light spirits of the council leaned in closer, "I wish to know what I've done to deserve so harsh a judgment," her voice trembled.

A bright light, not as brilliantly white as Orion's, but just as imposing, separated from the others and moved towards her.

Angelica couldn't say why, as these beings took only the form of light, but this guardian intimidated her more than Orion. She'd never been in the presence of the council before, but this light felt familiar.

"Angelica, you do understand you are not being punished but rewarded."

She knew he meant to calm her with his soothing tone but there was no comfort in his words. "It certainly *feels* like a punishment."

"Trust me; soon you'll see it as the reward it truly is."

"I doubt it," she mumbled and the guardian laughed.

The sound of his deep laughter struck a memory within her but she couldn't determine from when or where. She tried to see beyond the light that surrounded him but it was useless.

His voice was kind and sincere as he told her, "We know you have a great capacity to love others but on this level of existence you've chosen to block it."

"I haven't blocked it."

"Maybe not intentionally but you haven't allowed empathy for the mortals placed in your care either. Is that not true?"

Her silence was condemning but she couldn't completely deny it. Mostly, what she'd felt for those mortals was annoyance and frustration and very little compassion.

She looked away unable to defend herself.

"I know this seems harsh right now but this life will allow you to finally address the unfinished issues you've been harboring from…your last life."

Angelica heard the hesitation in his last words and her senses electrified with something she could almost grasp, some knowledge of that life that remained out of reach. Her eyes sharpened on him.

What did he know of her last life? She had no memory of it; she was allowed no memory of it.

"How am I supposed to know what baggage I'm carrying around if I'm not allowed that insight? Show me my last life and let me see if I can correct my empathy level without living this new life."

Orion moved but the light before her shook his head and addressed her question.

"It would not be a benefit to you now, trust us, this is the best solution. A new life with its opportunities to learn and grow is the best decision for you."

Angelica disagreed but felt the unanimous response to his words from all the light beings gathered round and knew it was futile to argue.

"If I do embrace this new life, will I embrace it with all that I am? Will I retain my understanding of self and the mysteries these mortals wonder of? Will I have full knowledge of all of this?"

There was swift movement among the council at her question but it was again the light being before her who answered.

"I am sorry Angelica, but you will not remember your spiritual existence here, nor any existence before this, only the new life you enter will be known to you."

"How is that fair?" Angelica demanded even more afraid of what was to come.

Orion stepped forward eclipsing the other being to inform her.

"Angelica, there is no more time to assure you of the rightness of our decision. You must accept it for the gift it is. It is time now for you to go."

Angelica felt overwhelming fear pulse through her at the finality of his words; she was trapped in a stunned silence as she desperately shook her head.

"I will see her through the storm."

She heard the familiar light being's request to Orion and heard the acceptable response but she was hearing it all as if in a distance.

"So be it."

Orion's thunderous words echoed through her as the atmosphere became charged with electrical currents.

Angelica felt herself being lifted into the air as easily as if she was a babe and in that moment, she knew she was.

The memory faded.

Angelica kept her focus on the bright lights above her, refusing to close her eyes, refusing to begin this new life.

"Please don't make me," she whispered sincerely but with little hope of being heard.

Her eyes widened when the nursery lights dimmed and a guardian's light appeared in the room. It was moving towards her. Hope lit in her heart; maybe her prayer had been heard.

Angelica felt a blanket of comforting warmth engulf her at the guardian's nearness.

"Are you here to take me back?"

"I'm here to try to erase your doubts and help you let go."

It was the familiar voice of the sympathetic guardian.

"I don't think that's possible," her dejected tone amplified her pain.

"Angelica, you are not being set adrift without any recourse; you will be watched closely and helped if absolutely necessary."

Her eyes widened with hurt pride.

"You mean I'll have an assigned spirit if I need one?"

"Yes, exactly," the guardian beamed with a bright light of reassurance.

Angelica felt the warm rays of comfort from him but she wasn't having any of it.

Her pride rose even higher as did her confidence. She'd show them she didn't need any of their help, she'd survive this life without it.

"Tell the council and most especially Orion not to bother; you won't have to send anyone to watch over me. I understand the limits of this life and I'll get through it by myself. I don't want any of their help."

The guardian, Dylan, smiled with admiration at her bravado, but of course she couldn't see it. He remembered her courage, and he remembered her. They'd both been mortal once, and once...she'd been his wife.

Dylan braced himself for the goodbye he didn't really want to give. He'd been fighting a strong sense of unease at the thought of her starting a new life...without him, but a guardian on his level had to separate from those feelings, had to think only of what was necessary for the attainment of perfection, had to know what was best for Angelica...and had to accept it.

He moved closer, closer than he should have and whispered, "It is time."

"Okay," her voice wasn't as sure as her earlier words had suggested, and she was sure he'd leave her now but to her amazement he began to take shape.

"Angel, I will miss you," Dylan whispered.

Angelica was stunned by the name he'd called her and the certainty that he'd called her that name before.

The familiar tone of his voice linked with his image as it became clearer, she focused sharply on his face.

He was very handsome; golden brown hair, framed a face both strong and tender and his sea green eyes burned with intensity and...love?

Suddenly, her eyes widened.

Recognition came to her like a fog dissipating in the sunlight. All her past life's memories surfaced fully and vividly. She remembered him and all the days of their life *together* and those memories sparked her long overdue anger.

"Dylan!"

Her voice rang out in accusation just as she felt herself lose consciousness.

Sleep came swiftly; no thoughts were left when she awoke, for the babe was overcome with a feeling of newness.

(Five years later)

Little Caroline Martinelli stood with the other five-year olds waiting to meet their new teacher and dreading their first day of kindergarten.

A boy stood behind her whimpering softly as two silly girls were laughing at him. Caroline wanted to punch them both.

"Hey, what's your name?" She turned around and asked the smaller boy.

"Justin," he said and tried to hide the fact that he'd been crying.

"Hello, Justin. I'm Caroline but you can call me Caro."

The boy smiled shyly at her.

Then Caro noticed the taller boy standing next to Justin, he looked like he wanted to punch the two silly girls too and it made her feel an instant friendship with him.

"Hi, I'm Caro," she said to the taller boy.

"I'm Jonathon but you can call me Jon," he smiled at her but he was still giving the two girls a steady stare of dislike.

The two girls had stopped laughing but one managed to send Caro a mean smile before they walked away.

Caro knew, with some innate wisdom, these girls would be trouble but she also knew that she could handle it. The world was a harsh place she decided, but she'd learn to live in it and she'd even help those she could along the way... like a guardian angel, she thought with a secretive smile, liking the title very much.

The bell rang loudly as parents hugged their children one last time before their new teacher, Mrs. Redmond, lined them up in pairs and had them follow her into the building.

Justin had been moved in front of them paired up with a little girl and Caro was paired with Jon and the two annoying girls were lined up behind them.

Caro heard them snickering but pretended not to hear. She knew 'If you ignore the fools they will get tired and leave you alone,' she didn't know how she knew it, but she knew it was true.

Jon was about to turn around and confront the two girls but Caro began talking to him about her favorite TV show.

It turned out to be his favorite show too and soon they truly didn't hear a thing behind them as they walked into their new classroom.

CHAPTER 2

(Twenty years later)

"Jon! Hurry up I don't want to be late for the appointment." Caro called out as she knocked on the door of the apartment across the hall from her, but before Jon answered she rushed back across the hall to finish getting ready.

Jonathon Forbes, Caro's best friend since kindergarten, walked across the hall and stood in her opened doorway watching her nervously rush around the room looking for something.

He was driving her to her job interview today in Manhattan and it was scheduled for one o'clock.

He looked at his watch, it was nearly noon.

"You'd better get a move on Caro if you don't want to be late. Traffic could be backed up."

"I'm almost ready," she said as she pulled up the couch cushion looking for her matching jacket but it wasn't there. She'd had it a moment ago but didn't see where she'd put it.

Jon leaned against the doorjamb and smiled as he watched her.

She was absolutely beautiful and he'd been in love with her since the first day of kindergarten when she'd befriended him. Of course, she didn't suspect his feelings because to her, he was just her 'good friend Jon.

She'd found her jacket under a chair where it had fallen and put it on, casually looking at her reflection in her wall mirror, she shook her head and made her beautiful golden hair fall into place perfectly, just as almost everything she commanded, it fell naturally to her desire. Jon's heart thudded with a familiar pain, one he'd almost learned to ignore...almost.

Caro didn't see her beauty and never fussed with her looks. Of course, in his opinion, she didn't need to, her vibrant blue-green eyes shone as clear as any precious stone, and her long golden hair fell in full waves to just below her shoulders. Her heart shaped face was blessed with a peaches and cream complexion, and the little dimple that winked at the corner of her mouth when she smiled could devastate any man.

Jon knew that well enough because that smile always took his breath away but, to his eternal frustration, she'd never looked at him with anything more than friendly affection.

Sometimes, when he was in the mood to soul search, he'd give in to wondering why.

He didn't think he was hard to look at. He stood six foot two with a broad shouldered build that was not too shabby. He certainly wasn't unappealing to women. At least, Marilyn had loved his laughing brown eyes, strong jaw, and well-defined mouth. Or so she'd said many times after a shared evening.

And then there was Brenda, who had loved to run her hands through his dark brown hair and admired the way it fell in a sexy wave across his forehead. At least that's what Brenda had told him. Beth on the other hand, had liked his muscles and Beth had been his latest girlfriend.

He'd had many relationships over the years but he couldn't seem to commit to any of them and, when he was truthful with himself, he admitted it was because none had ever come close to what he felt for Caro.

"Hey, stop standing there daydreaming Jon, I'm ready and we need to get going."

Caro grabbed his arm, ending his thoughtful pursuit of reasons why he wasn't attractive to her and they headed out the door.

"Did you remember to retype your resume?" Jon asked as they drove towards the Natural History Museum's Planetarium where Caro's interview was scheduled.

"Retype what? I didn't have all that much to put on it. A couple of waitress jobs while I was in college and an apprentice position at the Museum of Modern Art for one summer...Oh, and that clerk job in the gift shop at the Metropolitan Museum last Christmas. Certainly nothing that will wow them."

"You'll wow them, even without a resume." Jon assured her.

"Oh sure, and that's not just because you're my friend and you have to say things like that...Right?" Caro scrunched up her face as she always did when she mocked herself.

It made him want to kiss her but instead he turned his focus back on the road and ignored the urge as he told her honestly, "Believe me, friendship aside, your intelligence comes through in ordinary conversation. You have verve and sparkle and, even though I've known you forever, I still get blown away by it."

11

"Sure…and how much do you need? Are you short for this month's rent?" She laughed self-consciously and slid down further into the bucket seat of his car.

"I'm not kidding…but now that you mention it…I did pay for pizza last night. If you don't spring for dinner tonight I may have to go hungry just to pay next month's rent," he joked casually because it was easier than trying to be sincere. Sincerity could break his heart.

"Okay, I'll promise you this buddy, if I get the job today you can bet we are going to eat at the best restaurant in town tonight and…it will be my treat."

"Now there's some incentive. Let me see that little resume again, maybe I can punch it up before you go in."

Caro laughed shaking her head, "No thanks, I got this."

She was going to get this job on her own, completely on her own or not at all, she'd decided. She knew she'd be able to convince them how much she loved the study of space and time, because she'd loved anything to do with science and the universe since she was a child. Since, she'd been given her first telescope from her parents when she was six, to help her study the stars.

She had it covered when it came to her passion for space, but what she didn't have covered, was the experience.

"Here we are." Jon announced as he pulled up in front of the planetarium giving her a brilliant smile of encouragement.

"Thanks Jon." Caro did feel encouraged by his confidence in her. He was her anchor.

When she'd moved out on her own a year ago her parent's had let her go only when they'd realized Jon would be her neighbor, and could keep an eye on her. She loved that Jon was close by. He was her best friend forever. He'd been the brother she never had, the date when no one had asked her out, and the shoulder to cry on when friendships and dreams had fallen through. Jon was the one constant in her life and she could always depend on him to support her and make her feel secure, even if she failed.

"Good luck, and don't' worry about me…I'll just be circling around the block waiting for you," he added with a weary sigh for affect.

Caro laughed, "You're the best, you know that?" she kissed his cheek before opening the door to get out but turned back and said, "If I'm out of there in less than thirty, then don't bother to pick a restaurant but if I can last forty-five minutes then there's a good chance we're dining at 'Mezza Luna's' in Little Italy tonight, and on my treat."

"Oh sure, now I'll not only be driving around this exhaust fumed city but I'll be salivating the entire time…you realize now if you don't get this job, you'll have to cook me an Italian meal just to make up for this?"

"If you're willing to eat *my* cooking, I'd be glad to make you some 'Caro style' lasagna," she offered perkily.

Jon made a face that could only be described as ill.

"On second thought, we can just order in pizza again," he suggested quickly.

"Thanks for the opinion on my cooking," Caro laughed but knew it was true, she had no culinary skills. It was Jon who always had better results when he attempted it, "Well either way, we'll know soon enough if its pizza or the grand meal…here I go!"

She got out of the car and started walking toward the building.

Jon watched her hips sway gently as she walked away. She almost looked like an angel heading to heaven; the effect was magnified by the planets outlined in the large front paneled window of the museum's entrance. The thought caused goose bumps to rise on his arms and he had to shake his head to clear the image.

That was weird, he thought and pulled out into the traffic hoping it would be past the thirty minutes for her self-esteem, but he was still positive she could win them over in five.

(Council on High)

Dylan should have been happy to hear that Angelica's return to the physical world had taken off with fire. He *knew* he *should* be pleased...but he wasn't. What he was...was stagnant.

He had not moved spiritually beyond the last moment he'd seen her as Angelica, the moment when he'd allowed her to see him as he once was, her husband Dylan.

Since then, memories of their life together had remained stuck in his image recall and he'd been visualizing those days over and over again.

On his level of training, memories could be played before you, like a virtual reality movie but with depth and feelings added in for ultimate emotional recall.

Dylan had gained this privilege shortly after arriving on this side of life, but Angelica had not.

When she'd arrived, she'd been furious that death had taken her before she was ready to relinquish it, even more furious then when Dylan had been taken from her on the very day their only son was born to them.

After Dylan's death on that icy day, Angelica had given her whole life to raising their son and later to helping raise their grandchildren. She'd never gotten

14

over the loss of her husband and had never taken another chance on love.

The council would have returned her immediately to a new life if Dylan hadn't pleaded her case to let her stay. He'd offered to guide her to perfection with his shadowed direction, never allowing her to actually see him.

His request was granted but with a codicil.

If Angelica did not improve in one light cycle he would have to agree with the council to send her back and in the end that was exactly what he'd had to do.

All reports he'd seen on her progress showed Angelica was prospering in her new life.

He should be satisfied with those reports but he wasn't and that really concerned him.

Even more concerning, he was losing the desire to remain on the guardian plane without her, and the conflict was growing stronger within him.

Dylan tried to deter these feelings by telling himself she would return to *him* on her new life's completion but the images of their past life would not stop haunting him.

Once again, his past life materialized before him, life size, and in Technicolor, drawing out emotions he'd banked long ago.

He'd called her Angel, and they had been deeply in love and theirs was a perfect marriage. The summit of that love had been when she'd told him they would have a child in late December of the second year of their marriage.

That thought flipped the images forward.

No longer warm or comforting, these sights were sharp and edged with pain. It was the exact instant everything had ended for him and Angel.

Dylan didn't want to relive it but he couldn't shake away the image.

He was speeding along the road in his little silver sports car rushing home to Angel. Ten minutes earlier his neighbor had called him at work and told him she'd gone into labor.

He was desperate to reach her before the ambulance took her to the hospital and he'd thought he could make it easily home if he took the shortcut route, it was trickier but quicker than the safer route that would have taken longer, but he hadn't counted on the icy rain that began falling. He didn't estimate how fast the roads would become hazardous but he should have.

It had always been a bit of a risk with those hairpin turns on that mountain road…he should have driven slowly, and he should have taken the longer way home and stayed safe for her and the baby …he should have been more cautious that day but he needed to get to Angel and that was his last thought as the car veered over to the left side and down the ragged cliff.

Dylan winced seeing his car flipping over several times as it tumbled down.

He was locked into the image, unable to stop it, lost in the tragic ending of that life and heard nothing around him.

"Dylan I must commend you again on your insight," John walked up to Dylan with pages of a report in his hand and said, "Angelica is coming along splendidly. Have you seen the latest data on her new life?"

Dylan didn't respond.

"Dylan? Did you not hear me?" John spoke louder rattling the pages in front of Dylan.

Dylan blinked and shook his head scattering the images and reluctantly turned to John.

John was the closest to his level on the council and they were friends.

"Sorry, what can I help with?"

"Have you seen the latest reports on the newest assignments you've placed?" John held out the reports to him.

"No, I haven't," Dylan said with less than his usual enthusiasm. He couldn't release the feelings of loss that permeated deep into his spirit, but he had to force his attention back on what truly mattered…the attainment of perfection in all things.

He smiled at John and asked, "Are they good?"

John nodded, "I should say so. Jasmine has return to guiding the smallest children, and she is grateful to you for that. She always does a good job with innocent hearts."

"Yes, I know." Dylan agreed with a genuine smile.

"And ah… Desiree is most happy to be with the homeless. I can tell you that she has turned several from desperation. Confidentially Dylan, I have word that David has seen the reports on the newest guardians himself, and is most impressed with them. I wouldn't be surprised if he were to summon you personally since it was your insight to match the guardians to task in this fashion."

"I don't need congratulations John, it's what we do. It doesn't matter who had the vision, only that the vision was used."

"As always, you have the true light. I still have a lot to learn I'm afraid. I think my Wall Street days are too hard to forget," John said contritely then laughed, "I guess that's why I'm still the dimmest light on the council."

Dylan liked John's humor and smiled.

"Take my advice and don't try too hard to forget your last life. Take advantage of those memories; believe me they're necessary to help you move on," Dylan said the last ruefully, still feeling his own past hovering ominously around him.

"I'll take that advice," John agreed.

Dylan was about to ask for the report when a voice did summon him, and it was indeed the voice of David, The Supreme Supervisor.

CHAPTER 3

"I know that smile; it's your 'cat got the cream' smile, you got the job right?" Jon asked when Caro slid into the car's front bucket seat smiling happily.

"Yes! Yes! Yes!" She exclaimed then leaned over and kissed him full on the lips, "I got it," she whispered then sat back and sighed happily, "We *will* eat well tonight because we're going to celebrate my unbelievable good luck."

Caro snuggled deeper into the well worn leather of the seat as she held up her hand regally and commanded him, "Take us home Jon, we need to dress for a celebration dinner."

Jon felt the warmth from her kiss on his lips and wanted to pull her back and explore those tender lips further but knew it was just enthusiasm that prompted the kiss, he knew that, but his lips were burning all the same.

Maybe tonight he'd tell her how he felt. Maybe it was time to test their friendship and see where it could go? He turned and smiled at her.

"Your wish is my command, my lady. We'll dress for your success and paint the town in rainbows."

Caro gave him a brilliant smile and agreed, "That's exactly what we'll do."

*   *   *

The night was sheer magic.

The warm August breeze tantalized. The sultry smell of exotic dishes, coupled with the romantic blaze of candlelight, simply seduced.

Caro loved Little Italy, loved the atmosphere, and loved the people. The language was brisk and hearty, every word sounded like friendship and family.

She was glad Jon had come out with her tonight there wasn't anyone else she would have wanted to celebrate her new job with. Of course her parents were proud and happy for her but they would have made the evening more staid, more formal.

What she wanted was comfort and fun and Jon was the best choice for both tonight.

He was her *amico comico*, her funny friend. And she didn't have to restrain her exuberance with him because he was like family...like Little Italy, carefree and fun!

"So, are you ready to order now or do I have to starve for another fifteen minutes while you drink in the sights and sip your wine?" Jon teased.

He knew she never made hasty decisions. Everything in life was paramount with her even ordering a meal. Sometimes she drove him crazy with her perfectionism but, if he did end up in the land of crazy, it would be worth it if he ended up there with her.

Caro smiled impishly at him and picked up her menu.

"Maybe the lasagna?" she asked peering over the top of her menu at him.

Jon smiled but said nothing; she was nowhere near a decision. He folded his arms on the table to wait.

"No, Lasagna would be too heavy. Don't you think?' she answered herself and looked back down at the menu.

The waiter walked towards them but Jon shook his head. It would be awhile before the lady would need his pen and pad.

The waiter retreated discreetly to fill the wine glass at another table.

"Maybe a chicken entree...let me see...should I have the Chicken Francese? That sounds so good...but that might be too lemony. I'm not up for lemony," she shook her head.

Jon sat back and sipped his wine not engaging at all in her indecision.

Caro looked over her choices again.

"Maybe, Chicken Marsala. Yes, that's exactly what I want," she looked up at Jon nodding her head.

"I'm going to have the Chicken Marsala with a side of penne in garlic and oil and tossed with broccoli flowerets. Don't you think that sounds deliciously perfect?" She asked putting down her menu and folding her arms across it.

"I'm ready now. Do you see our waiter?"

"I'm sorry Caro, he and the cook have gone home they gave up waiting for you to decide." Jon said matter-of-factly.

"Very funny, just call him over...please, I'm starving," Caro whispered and her stomach grumbled adding sound effects to her words.

Jon laughed and signaled the nearest waiter to request their server.

The meal was superb, and Caro was animated with happiness talking about her new job's responsibilities.

Jon hadn't yet found an opening to comfortably tell her his feelings, but he was still hopeful that tonight would present an opportunity.

"I know it's just an entry-level position and I'll mainly be escorting school groups through the planetarium but part of the time I'll get to sit in with some very prominent astrophysicists during their meetings. I'll be keeping the minutes as they discuss their current research and findings. I'm pinching myself that I actually have this job."

"That's great Caro. Did you tell them you'll be going for your masters in astrophysics?"

"Well, I mentioned it but of course I don't have any working background yet. Face it, I'm fresh out of college with only sales clerk jobs to show for experience, how impressed could they be?"

"You did have that summer internship with the research program at the University of Hawaii's Institute of Astronomy."

"Yes, and that was three years ago. It was a wonderful summer and working with a professional astrophysicist on the formation of galaxies was amazing. Having the use of the Haleakala observation telescope in Maui for viewing the planets was a true plus and something I'll never forget but it was an internship. I still haven't had a job in the field."

"You're too hard on yourself Caro. They did hire you. They must have seen something that impressed them."

"I don't know about my impressing them but I'll learn so much just being in the same room with those esteemed professors. Jon, they could have made me the janitor and I would have been ecstatic just cleaning the rooms while they talked shop."

Jon leaned forward and placed his hand over hers, "You would be the most beautiful janitor they'd ever seen."

Caro blushed, "Why thank you Jon, you even made it sound some what romantic."

He wasn't surprised, romance was definitely on his mind and maybe the moment to tell her was now.

"Caro I'm happy your wish is coming true, and tonight…tonight I'm wondering if there's even a slight chance that mine could too." Jon's eyes were sharp and intensely focused on her.

It was a penetrating look Caro hadn't seen before and her heart jumped at the thought that he was unhappy.

"What's wrong, Jon?" Is it your comic strip? Please don't give up on 'Little Cal n' Ivy' I just know you're going to make that Sunday edition soon," she said sincerely covering his hand with hers. "You're an amazing artist and writer; and you know your captions always make me laugh."

She loved 'Little Cal n' Ivy' and she was not alone in her praise, he'd received some critical acclaim and won several awards for the comic strip.

Jon shook his head and turned his hand over so he could hold hers.

"I'm not talking about Cal and Ivy. It isn't my *job* I'm thinking of at all, it's…" he hesitated, if Caro hadn't sensed his meaning and if he bared his soul to her, and she didn't feel the same, she'd feel responsible for his pain, after she let him down nicely of course. Should he risk their friendship? Suddenly the timing felt off. He shrugged and let go of her hand, "Forget I said anything, this is *your* night we're celebrating, your happiness and no serious conversations allowed," he laughed softly at himself, and if it had been a bit self mocking she didn't seem to notice.

"Jon, I didn't think there was anything you couldn't tell me so if it isn't your comic strip then is something wrong between you and Beth?"

"Beth?" Jon had to concentrate to remember who Beth was, that's how much Caro affected him, "Yeah, sure it's Beth," he shrugged. He could at least give her a partial truth, "I'm tired of fast relationships that have no meaning. I want someone I can love for a lifetime, someone who can share my dreams and I know for sure, that isn't Beth."

"I see. She isn't ready to commit to you and you wouldn't pressure her into a commitment."

"No, Caro you didn't hear me. That isn't what I said. I said it *isn't* Beth," he stressed the point but he could see she wasn't listening and he knew why and nothing he said now would stop where her thoughts were going.

"You're so considerate of others Jon, not like…" her words trailed off and in her mind she was back in college. When she let her self remember that day, it always seemed like it happened yesterday. It was the day everything changed in how she looked at love and commitment. She hadn't been ready to commit a lifetime to Mitch, commitment being the word that froze her that day and ever since, and she couldn't even say why.

Jon groaned annoyed with himself that he'd put her thoughts back into that day.

"Caro, please don't go there," he whispered but it was too late. Her gaze was fixed on the candlelight and she was obviously reliving that moment. He'd become well acquainted with that look and it took him back too.

For months after Mitch left for Boston, Caro had looked like that.

Mitch Ryder had truly loved Caro and Caro had claimed she loved him too. The relationship between them had started in their senior year of high school and lasted until just before graduation from New York University, until the day Mitch proposed to her.

Jon had never seen Caro afraid of anything as she was of that engagement ring and he never understood her fear that night. His memory of that day was as sharp and clear too.

He'd been cramming for a calculus test all evening and had just fallen into a deep sleep when the pounding on his door woke him up. He jumped out of bed and stubbed his toe on the nightstand. Cursing loudly, and muttering that whoever it was had better be in a life or death situation or they soon would be. He hobbled to the door but when he opened it he lost all anger.

Caro stood on his doorstep shaking and sobbing. He was afraid to ask who'd died but before he could utter a word she ran into his apartment.

"Jon, I can't do it. I just can't," Caro beseeched him with pain in her eyes.

Jon didn't have a clue what she couldn't do but he nodded and gently led her to the couch. When they sat down she collapsed against him.

"Why did he have to ask me? Why? Things were perfect just the way they were. Perfect!"

She told him with tears in her eyes.

"What did he want you to do?" Jon's hand fisted and he was ready to defend her honor. He wasn't sure what had been asked of her, but it had to be something pretty sick for her to be this distraught. Mitch would get a strong answer from him tomorrow. He'd supply him with two times five hard felt answers. His hands balled into tight fists.

25

"What did he want you to do Caro?" he repeated in a soothing voice, even though his blood was boiling.

"He wants me to..." she shook her head and sobbed harder.

"He wants you to what?" Jon leaned closer expected her to whisper the awful words.

"He wants me to marry him!" She said forcefully and pulled away from him as she stood up.

The words hung in the air and Jon wondered what he was missing here?

"He wants to marry you," he repeated slowly, "and that's a bad thing?"

Caro didn't answer she just nodded her head and sat back down on the couch.

Jon stared at her not knowing what to say. He'd thought she liked Mitch and had just recently accepted the fact that she probably loved Mitch. It hadn't been easy for him to let go of his dreams of Caro and him, but he loved her so much that her happiness was important to him but now, he didn't know what to think, and he still didn't know what was wrong.

"Why is it a bad thing Caro, if you love him? You do love him don't you?"

Caro looked away. It was a few minutes before she answered.

"Yes...I mean...I think I love him...as much as I know what love is anyway," she said derisively.

"So you *don't* love him?"

"Maybe I do...but...I just can't commit to forever. I'm not ready to trust in love lasting that long and I can't give anyone that kind of power over me. Not yet...and before you ask me why...I don't know why I feel this way. Maybe I'm just not ready to marry."

"Then tell him that."

"I told him. I begged him to give me some time," she put her hand in her coat pocket and pulled out a ring box. She opened it and flashed the bright stone at Jon's face, "He gave me this ring and only tonight to think about it."

The diamond glistened in the lamplight.

Jon looked at the ring then back at her.

Her eyes began filling with tears but it was the stark fear on her face that concerned him.

"Caro, what's really wrong here? You know you're not acting rational about this."

"I know," she said staring at the ring.

What was wrong with marriage? Jon wondered. He didn't think her parents had a bad one but maybe there was something he didn't know.

"What are you so afraid of?"

"I wish I knew, but I really don't. I only know that the thought of marriage makes me want to run away. I don't think its Mitch...not really. When he asked me at first I was thrilled but in the next second I was sick with fear...I had this uncomfortable feeling, it just bubbled up from deep within me and ...I have no reason for it."
"What was the feeling?"

"This is going to sound crazy but somewhere deep inside me I know it's true."

"What?"

"Okay, but if I tell you, don't judge." Her eyes pleaded with him.

"Have I ever?"

"No," Caro smiled, "Okay, the fear is this...I believe if I marry *anyone* it'll end badly, very badly. It sounds so ridiculous to say this out loud but somehow I know it's true. I'll never be able to make that forever vow."

"Maybe you're not ready to share your life today but to say not ever..."

"No, it's true, I know it...not now and not ever...I don't think this feeling will change but...I don't know where this is coming from either so...Maybe in time...but I don't know."

"You just need to fall for the right guy."

She smiled, "Like you?"

Jon was about to agree when she started crying again.

"You should have seen Mitch he was so hurt," she said with a quivering smile.

"If he loves you and I'm sure he does because..." Jon leaned forward and wiped away the tears on her cheeks, "no one could resist loving someone as open and caring as you. Tell him to wait...give you time to figure out your feelings."

"I tried to. I tried to explain how I felt but he doesn't understand me, not like you do. He doesn't listen like you do either. He only heard that I don't love him enough to say yes."

"When he thinks it over tonight, I'm sure he'll call you in the morning and give you more time."

"No, he won't. He gave me an ultimatum and I have to call him tomorrow, he isn't calling me...he won't understand my feelings any better tomorrow." Caro closed the black velvet jeweler's box and held it out to Jon. "Would you give this back to him for me, I can't face him, I'll write a letter you can give him."

Jon shook his head and closed his hand over the box she held moving it back to her, "Caro you can't ask me to be your messenger, not in this. This isn't grade school and we're not talking about passing little love notes."

It was hard to deny her anything but this was something he knew he couldn't do for her. "Please," she whispered and moved the box closer to him.

"I'm sorry Caro, but he deserves to hear it from you."

She nodded sadly, "You're right, I'll tell him but he isn't going to wait for me," she whispered and put the box back in her coat pocket.

"Then he's a fool." Jon murmured as she leaned her head on his shoulder and he'd held her that way through most of the night.

*   *   *

The candle on the table sputtered out and both Jon and Caro realized they'd let the memory take over their thoughts.

"Sorry," she gave him a slight smile, "I didn't mean to put such a sad note on tonight. I've been over Mitch for a very long time and I know it wasn't true love between us but that day...that day was life defining and I can't get over those feelings."

"Why is that Caro?" Jon asked, still puzzled by her reactions that night.

Her eyes became pensive and she shrugged, "I know it's irrational to be so sure of something without a reason, but it's *never* gone away. I just know I don't ever want to take a chance on forever with anyone."

"Caro, you shouldn't say never...maybe you just need to find your soul mate."

"Soul mate," Caro laughed at the expression, "You Jonathon Forbes, you believe in soul mates?"

"Yes, I do...very much," Jon smiled wickedly and picked up her hand and kissed it making her smile.

"You're the best remedy for me, Jon. Why can't I just fall in love with you? We've never have a bad day or even a little misunderstand between us."

"Yeah, why can't you?" Jon's heart pounded and he squeezed her hand. Was this the time to declare his feelings?

Caro kissed his cheek and whispered, "I love you and our friendship is the best thing in my life and with this new job I'm where I've always wanted to be."

He took her hand and decided to open his heart, "Caro, I'm happy for you and –"

"Thank you Jon, I couldn't be happier than I am now and this opportunity solidifies my reasoning."

"What?"

"That a commitment would only have ruined this chance, so again it proves I'm better off not married."

Jon wanted to strongly disagree but he didn't. He let go of her hand and sat back, "I'm glad you're happy Caro."

"Best friends forever?" she held out her pinky to him as they had done since grade school.

"And ever," he finished the childhood promise and linked his pinky around hers.

It certainly wasn't the declaration of love he'd wanted to make but Caro was gun-shy on long-term commitments and even if she didn't know the reason behind her fear, her fear was real. He hoped in time she'd get over that fear and open her heart to loving someone completely, and if he had to find a candidate for that love... well... best friends did make the best husbands.

At least, that's what Julia had told him when she'd asked him to marry her in sixth grade. He'd turned her down of course.

He had already set his sights on Caro and they'd never wavered once.

CHAPTER 4

(Council on High)

A bright, golden light engulfed Dylan. He was absorbed into the energy of goodness it emitted. When the bright light faded, a large imposing figure of a man, dark haired, with piercing blue eyes stood before him.

David smiled welcoming him, "Dylan, I am truly impressed by the field work you have been overseeing."

"Thank you," Dylan said a little self consciously, unsure of what to say to the guardian who sat so close to the top.

"No need to feel awed, you have moved along in the right path and perhaps are deserving of a little help in the best direction."

"I'd be grateful for any advice you can offer me."

"Good. I'm glad to hear that, as I do have some for you," he motioned Dylan to follow him out of the aura filled space of light and into a garden of exotic plants.

Dylan could smell their fragrances and he felt warm sunshine on his face. It was like life and the sunshine felt good, his skin tingled with sensations…Skin?

Dylan looked down and saw he too had taken form, but why and for what purpose? He wondered as he followed David into the garden.

The smell of the blooms around him stirred a memory and he closed his eyes and breathed deeply, he recognized it immediately…Hawaii, where he and Angelica had spent their honeymoon.

"Would you like some refreshment?"

The deep voice drew Dylan back and his eyes snapped open. David was motioning to a moving bar making its way over to them, and it was being propelled by a flowery shirted waiter.

"No, thank you," Dylan shook his head as he eyed his superior curiously and David's deep laugh threw him even further off guard.

"Relax, Dylan. Pleasures are acceptable and I have always found Hawaii to be most pleasurable."

"So we *are* in Hawaii? Are we real time?" Dylan's confusion grew.

David didn't answer the questions, he turned to the waiter as he handed him a tall, ice blue glass with a small drink umbrella sticking out of the top of it.

David sipped the drink and smiled before turning back to Dylan.

"Are you sure you won't try one? This is a most refreshing elixir, not of the alcoholic variety enjoyed to excess in life but, none the less, it is potent in its way. If you try it, you'll see why it is enjoyed only on certain plateaus," he said then took a long sip from the tall glass and sighed, "Ah, it is a most warmth inducing drink, thirst quenching, and soul satisfying, but you must be ready to experience it," he said with a challengingly smile.

Dylan had an impression of an energy drink commercial and nearly laughed at the thought but David's next question wiped the thought of laughing from his mind.

"So Dylan have *you* ever been to Hawaii?" David eyed him over the top of his drink umbrella.

"Ah…yes, I have," he answered hesitantly, unsure of where the conversation was leading.

"Do you remember it well?" David asked casually as he handed Dylan a tall jade green glass, even though he had not requested one.

It chilled at the touch, Dylan looked down into the drink in his hand and the memories swirled up at him.

"Mai Tai's…We drank Mai Tai's on the beach at sunset," Dylan smiled at the memory and took a small sip of the elixir in the glass and was suddenly lost in vivid images.

"The sun was setting behind her but the brilliant hues were a dim background to her beauty. She wore a red bikini and after the third Mai Tai we-," Dylan stopped and shook his head. What was he saying? "Sorry… I don't know what that was."

David's deep laugh rang out," That was conscience, Dylan. Say hello to it. It has been trying to talk to you for some time now and you *have been* avoiding it. Haven't you?"

"I don't understand."

David nodded, "I know your desire to attain perfection has been your priority and it is noted, but it is obvious that you have been torn since Angelica returned to the cycle of life, could it be that perhaps she was not the only one who had unfinished lessons in life to confront?"

33

"No! No, not at all," Dylan shook his head emphatically, "When I arrived here, I was granted this level of training. I didn't request it but I embraced it wholeheartedly. Would it have been offered if I wasn't ready for it?"

The sapphire blue of David's eyes locked on the troubled green of Dylan's as he spoke. "Many offers are made to us and we pick and choose what feels best, but that does not mean there was not another way to go. Remember Dylan, free will is always present."

"So I wasn't ready for this?"

"Only you can answer that."

Dylan stared at him knowing it was true. Only he could answer, but did he want to? He hadn't stopped thinking about Angelica since she'd left but he knew she would return to him at her life's end anyway...wouldn't she? Of course, he wished her success in her new life...but could he really be harboring a desire to go to her? Live a full life, possible one that ended better? But why would he want that pain again? Why would anyone?

"What pain Dylan?"

Dylan looked at David, shocked that he had heard his thoughts, or had he said them out loud? He wasn't sure.

"I don't know what I meant. I guess that...life is painful. Feelings are intense."

"Yes, but feelings can be pleasure as well as pain can't they?" David advised sagely but he didn't wait for Dylan's answer, with the last word he dispersed into so much sparkling sunlight it momentarily blocked out all else.

When the sparkling mist evaporated, Dylan realized he'd been left alone to ponder the question.

He was being given a chance to choose his next direction but he really didn't want to go back to life. He was more than ready to proceed from here. He'd earned this and was ready to attain final perfection…wasn't he?

Suddenly, the garden melted away and the drink vanished from his hand.

Dylan was now standing fully on the beach.

"Honolulu," he breathed the name as he felt the tropical breezes.

Yes, he knew it immediately. He was standing on Waikiki Beach and he could see Diamond Head in the distance.

He walked toward the ocean's edge and fell to his knees on the soft sand.

The warm grains moved to accommodate him as he lay down on the soft bed, breathing in the smell of the sea salted air.

He had to admit, it was one of the most stimulating life smells.

He rolled over onto his back and closed his eyes, feeling the sun's rays on his face, drawing in the warmth of it while his hands sifted through the sand at his sides.

He felt like a kid again and it felt unburdening. It was fun…Fun?

He had forgotten that too, forgotten that feeling of freedom like one has in childhood.

Suddenly, he heard sounds all around him. Sounds of a beach filled with people. Children's voices squealed with laughter as they played in the surf and radios blared out summer songs.

He chuckled, knowing that David was giving him the 100 watts of temptation now but he could take it. He'd let the sun warm him and the sounds of summer lull him into peacefulness. He would still request to stay but that didn't mean he couldn't enjoy this moment before he did.

A cold wet drop of water landed smack on his belly and Dylan jumped up.

Looking down at the droplet of water running down his stomach, he saw that he was in his swim trunks. A pair he hadn't seen since his honeymoon.

"Did I get you wet? Sorry Hon."

She flopped down next to him on the checkered blanket that hadn't been there a minute ago and she turned to him with a sexy smile that stopped his heart.

"Don't look so scared I won't devour you here on the beach; I can wait till we go upstairs. We still have three more days in honeymoon paradise." She winked at him then leaned down and brushed a kiss across his lips.

Dylan wanted to pull her in and deepen the teasing sample.

"Angel?" he whispered doubting the vision even as he breathed in the scent of her, she'd always made him think of summer sunshine and sea breezes.

"You sound surprised. Were you expecting someone else?" She looked at him oddly.

"No! I just … I just haven't seen you in awhile," he gave her a lopsided grin but his heart was pounding and he was sure she could hear it.

"Yeah, like you didn't see me just fifteen minutes ago when I went to swim in the ocean and you were too tired to join me," she laughed but her expression changed to worry at the shocked look in his eyes. "Maybe you've had too much sun. Are you feeling all right? You don't look well honey."

She reached out her hand and smoothed his hair back from his forehead checking if he had a fever.

Her touch was his undoing.

The beach wasn't the 100-watt temptation *she was* and lord save him she was wearing that red bikini!

"I'm fine Angel...just needed you," he whispered and took her hand from his brow and pulled her down to him.

The kiss magnified the days and nights of their honeymoon and the undeniable desire he had to be with her.

CHAPTER 5

The third grade class visiting the museum was fully energized and Caro was power walking to keep up with them because the three mothers and two teachers, who were chaperoning the group, seemed to be on their own field trip, laughing and lollygagging far behind the class.

Thankfully, the tour was nearing the end. She smiled at the thought and directed the class tour towards the museum's theater for a thirty-minute space show. The best part of this show was she didn't have to stay with the tour during it.

She ushered the class through the open theatre doors and felt revived just dreaming of the strong cup of coffee she would be having while the little angels were occupied.

The last child and teacher entered and she turned to step away from the theatre door but stopped when she heard someone calling for her to hold the door.

Caro saw two of the parental chaperones walking briskly towards her as the automatic doors began to close. She had to stand against one of the doors to force it to stay open for them.

The two parents were giggling like schoolgirls as they passed her and Caro really wanted to tell them to be quiet but instead she smiled sweetly and let the door close a shade quicker than she should have, bumping the butt of the last mom to enter.

It was a small satisfaction but a satisfaction all the same.

Caro reached the sanctuary of the café and smiled at her friend Nancy who worked there as a waitress. Nancy and Caro had been best friends through grade school but they'd gone to different high schools and lost touch for awhile. Now Nancy served lunch at the Terrace Café in the day and went to Pace University at night hoping to finish her degree in Business Law.

It was a pleasant and welcome surprise to have her old friend working at the museum.

"Make it a double strong dose of caffeine please," Caro requested as she slid into an empty seat at a corner table.

The slim, dark haired waitress nodded with a knowing smile, "Are you sure you can take it, Caro? My double dose is more caffeine than most coffee addicts can take."

"Hit me with it, I need it," she begged as she laid her head tiredly down on her arms.

Today with her first school group nearly complete she needed that boost of caffeine to calm her jangling nerves.

"You sure look beat. Those kids ran you ragged today huh?"

Nancy poured the fresh steaming coffee into a mug and placed it before her nearly comatose friend.

"Ran me, dragged me, and stomped on my remains. I have a whole new respect for grade school teachers."

"Hah…when the middle school students start coming in…you'll be begging for the little ones." Nancy predicted and walked away laughing.

Caro raised her head and wondered what had she signed on for?

She poured cream into her cup and stirred absently hoping the time would go slowly, she had twenty minutes before she had to reclaim the group for the final phase of the tour, the Museum's gift shop.

Just the thought of what was to come had her cringing and draining the strong cup of java in nearly one long, life restoring sip.

"Rough day?"

The deep voiced question was so close it made her jump and some coffee splashed out of her cup onto the table. Caro looked up and held the gaze of a tall, dark haired, older man she didn't recognize.

"Sorry I didn't mean to scare you. I believe you sat in on our meeting last evening Ms. Martinelli. I'm David." He held his hand out to her.

Caro stared in awe at his brilliant smile, it blinded her for a second and then she took in his perfect features and his piercing blue eyes. How did she miss noticing him last night? If he were at that meeting, she certainly *would* have noticed him.

David laughed softly at her zombie like stare, and tried again to introduce himself.

"I'm David McKay, Professor of Physics," he said still holding his hand out to her.

Caro smiled back at him, "Nice to meet you," she said and finally shook his hand and in that touch she suddenly remembered him speaking at the meeting last night, she hadn't had that memory a moment ago, but now the memory was vivid.

"Yes, I do remember you Professor McKay and you were absolutely brilliant. Your research was positively spellbinding and ...Uh...would you like to join me?" she realized her manner's a little late and promptly nodded to the empty chair at her table.

David laughed a deep, soul satisfying laugh but shook his head.

"Regretfully, I can not but I do appreciate the offer."

"Are you sure?" her hope filled voice surprised her, she thought she sounded like a child begging a parent to stay and felt the blush starting to warm her cheeks. Thankfully, Professor McKay didn't seem to notice.

"I wish I could but I'm needed somewhere else...before I leave, I was wondering Caroline. It is Caroline? Have I remembered your name correctly?"

"Yes, but I prefer Caro. What were you wondering?"

David nodded, "Caro, it is. I was wondering how you're acclimating to your new...job?"

"Oh," she smiled happily, "I love it here. I've loved science and anything to do with the universe since I was very young and I still can't believe I was hired to work here. It's an unexpected gift; a true blessing... it's like a miracle."

David's sapphire blue eyes crinkled as he smiled at her.

"Nice choice of words, Caro. I think the entire universe is a blessing," his eyes sparkled like stars and held hers in a searching look as he asked, "Do you like Astronomy?"

"Yes, I do," she murmured locked in contact with those celestial eyes.

"Do you star gaze?"

"I have a small telescope I use to look at the night sky but it has to be a very clear night to get any viewing from it. It isn't very powerful," she answered as if they were old friends.

David leaned down to her, his infinitely blue eyes level with hers as he spoke.

"I have found that the naked eye is more powerful than any telescope for some kinds of viewing. I think you should try it."

"View the night sky with just with my eyes? I really don't think I'd see very much," she laughed kindly but his eyes pierced hers and she was held in a powerful sea of blue as he elaborated on his theory.

"On a clear night Caro, look deep into the heavens with nothing but your eyes and you may be very surprised at what you *can* see and what you'll understand."

His deep voice hypnotized her and she could almost believe she saw the heavens in his eyes. She nodded promising solemnly, "I will."

"Good," he said decisively and straightened to his full height breaking the eye contact.

A satisfied smile played on his face as he glanced at his watch, "I do have to go now; I have a class of new students waiting."

"I'm so sorry you can't stay longer." She was sincerely disappointed, something about him made her feel at peace with …everything.

"I have enjoyed our conversation very much Caro and if I may impart one more suggestion?" His eyes held hers and at her enthusiastic nod he continued, "If you find the time, there is an amateur astronomy group that meets on the planetarium's terrace one night a week. I think you might enjoy attending one of their gatherings."

"I'll certainly look into that. Thank you Professor McKay."

"Just David, Caro…call me David…most do."

His smile was a brilliantly blinding light that froze her with its beauty, and Caro had to swallow hard before she could say a proper goodbye.

She stared at the café door long after he had gone wondering if what had just happened had been real. It had felt profound and she didn't want to let go of the calm serenity he'd made her feel.

Nancy stepped to Caro's table breaking into her trance.

"Wow! He was beyond handsome, completely off the Richter scale of good looks. Who is he?" She asked as she refilled Caro's cup.

"Doesn't he ever have lunch here?" Caro asked still staring at the door.

"Not that I know. I've never seen him before. Believe me…*him* I would have remembered," she added a few more drops of hot coffee to Caro's nearly full cup.

Caro looked up at her oddly, "Are you sure? He's an astrophysicist and I think he was at a panel debate last night, though suddenly the memory isn't so clear."

"Hmmm…Well, I'm positive he's not one of the professors I've seen here before but trust me, I'll keep an eye out for him from now on. Great looking guys like that are not too easy to find," Nancy wiggled her eyebrows at Caro.

Caro nodded in complete agreement and picked up her cup. She took another long sip of the bitter brew and glanced at the clock on the café wall.

The conversation with Professor McKay had only taken five minutes? That didn't feel right but the clock touted otherwise.

She smiled gratefully; she still had fifteen minutes before the sky show ended. Fifteen minutes of quiet solitude before she'd have to go back to the rambunctious group of third graders.

Nancy returned and slipped a small piece of dark chocolate cake in front of her.

"Here this should help revive your energy," she patted Caro's shoulder before sauntering off to offer a cup of coffee courage to another tour guide who'd stumbled into the café grumbling about ill-mannered parents and under authoritative teachers.

*   *   *

The Museum's Shop was filled with wonderful items and the children wanted to see and touch each and every one of them.

The Teachers had organized the chaos by placing the children in small groups of ten to enter the shop; each group was led by one of the parents and was given ten minutes to shop.

Caro walked along the store's parameters helping children with items they wanted to see that were too high up on the shelves and answering question when she could.

She scanned the room to see where she might be needed next when she noticed one little boy standing alone by a shelf of books.

He was looking longingly up at a book about the night sky. It was very high up on the shelf so Caro approached him and asked if he'd like to see it.

The small boy shrugged his shoulders and put his hands into his pockets.

Caro took the book off the shelf, knelt down to his size, and opened it.

"Do you know what's on this page?"

Shyly, he pointed out all the constellations he could name and that was quite a few. Caro was very impressed by his knowledge and turned the next page.

The boy was fascinated by the pictures of the Milky Way Galaxy and the Virgo Cluster. His eyes were wide with wonder as he read the text beneath them.

Caro definitely shared his interest in the subject. His reaction reminded her how she had felt as a child when she looked through her little telescope for the first time at that endless night sky and realized the immenseness of the universe above her.

The school children all wore school bus shaped nametags around their necks with their first name and their school's name printed in block letters.

Caro looked at the boy's name tag, his name, Michael, was neatly printed on it.

"Do you like this book Michael?" she asked and smiled at the boy's enthusiastic nod.

"Did you want to buy it?" She held it out to him.

The boy's eyes shifted away and he shook his head.

Caro knew then, he really wanted the book but he might not have the money to buy it. She remembered when her Dad had bought her a book very similar to this one when she was about Michael's age and it had fueled her dreams. She could see that Michael felt the same way about the stars as she had and she decided right then to come up with a way to give this book to him.

She heard the teacher telling this group their time was up.

The teacher, a Miss Flora, her name printed on her teacher's bus tag, addressed the children

"Attention students, you will have to make your purchases now, no more time to shop. We have to be on time for the buses. Hurry up now."

Caro watched Michael walk out of the store, his little shoulders hunched dejectedly and it was then she quickly formed a plan.

After some quick calculations, she picked up the book and a few other items. She knew with her twenty percent discount she could buy each of the students a small telescope key chain, and as a bonus she would be awarding one child the book about the night sky.

It was going to be a fixed contest but she was sure she'd be forgiven.

All of the groups had finished shopping and were standing on line to leave when Caro stepped out of the gift shop. She saw that all of the other children held a museum bag tightly in their hands, all except Michael.

Caro smiled at the teacher but addressed the children

"I wanted to let you all know that you've been a wonderful group of students today and I'll let you in on a little secret…you were my very first tour group and because of that I'd like to make this a special day for all of us before your tour ends, if I may?" She looked to Miss Flora for agreement.

The teacher nodded and when Caro called them to her she let the children gather around her.

"I'd like all of you to play a game with me. Everyone will get a thank you gift for playing, but one of you will win a special surprise. Do you want to play?"

The children yelled their enthusiastic agreement and the teachers had to quiet them down. After they'd quieted, Caro explained the game.

She asked them to think of a word that had something to do with the universe and she would think of a word too. The child that guessed the word that she was thinking of would win the special surprise.

The children agreed to the rules and the game began.

"Mars," guessed the first child and Caro shook her head.

"Gemini," said another and again Caro shook her head.

It went twice around the class until Michael stood before her for a second time.

"Milky Way," he said shyly.

"Yes!" Caro cheered and held out the book to him. "You've won! You must be psychic; how did you ever guess what I was thinking?"

Michael shook his head unsure of how he did it, but his eyes were alight with happiness. His classmates cheered for him. After all, they all had had a chance to win the game but Michael was the only one who'd guessed correctly.

Miss Flora, caught Caro's attention, her eyes were bright with knowledge and what appeared to be tears. She mouthed a sincere thank you to Caro before she briskly called the children to line up telling them it was time to leave and they had to hurry.

The Parents helped the teachers gather the children in pairs and walked the group out of the museum to the waiting buses.

Caro followed the group out and just before they boarded the buses, as she had promised, she gave each of the children a telescope keychain for playing the game.

Michael looked back at her just before he got on the bus and waved happily while hugging his book tightly in his arm.

She waved back wondering how could she ever have thought those kids were a handful? They were wonderful, each one a little angel and she absolutely loved this job!

She kept waving until the bus was out of sight.

"Hey, Caro!"

She heard a familiar voice call her name and turned to see Jon sprinting towards her. She smiled and motioned him into the building.

"What are you doing here?"

"I had to drop off my comic strip to the paper and I actually found a parking space a block from here… I thought maybe you'd like a ride home."

"Would I like a ride home?" She held out one hand as if weighing the thought, "a nice comfortable car ride or," she held out her other hand, "the sticky, hot air of the subway cars?" Moving each hand up and down as she thought about her prospects she playfully shrugged and said, "Gee Jon, that's a real tough one. I don't know," she tilted her head and furrowed her brow as if she really had to contemplate it.

"Well, if it's that hard a decision I certainly don't want to fry your brain, so I'll just let you go home your usual way," Jon turned to go and laughed when Caro grabbed his arm to stop him.

"You do and I'll never speak to you again Jonathon Forbes," she laughed when he turned around, "If you wait in the café and have a cup of coffee, I'll ask Nancy to slip you a piece of the chocolate cake they have today. You'll be in heaven when you taste it and by the time you're done, I should be ready to go."

"Bribery…? Well, I'd say I can't be bribed but…where my stomach's concerned I can't control its greed. You win, but that cake better be all my stomach thinks it is or I won't be responsible for my actions. I may have to drive with the air conditioner off and the windows open."

Caro laughed, "Trust me. It's the best. See you in about thirty minutes."

It was typical of Jon to think of her, to stop by to take her home. He was always thoughtful and she could not imagine what her life would have been like without him in it and she never wanted to find out. At that thought she stopped short.

What she was feeling for Jon suddenly felt a lot like a commitment. She didn't want a tomorrow without him in it and she really *could* see spending forever with him. They'd been best friends for so long why wouldn't they be together forever…because friends could find someone else to love and leave you and she'd never thought about that before, she never thought Jon would ever be out of her life…but he could be…and suddenly her heart felt heavy. Did she feel more for Jon than friendship? It was suddenly possible she did.

*   *   *

(Council on High)

Dylan watched the dark clouds gathering. The bright flash of electrical current boded ill for the guides awaiting the council. He'd never failed at any assignment given him since the day he'd arrived on this plane, so gray clouds of judgment had never formed above his head, but lately he felt as if they should.

He listened as the council discussed the guides gathered before them, requesting some be given new chances in training, while others were to be sent back to the lower plane of life, like Angelica had been.

Angelica, he sighed. Her image burned through his thoughts. She too had stood before the council and the gray that day had been impenetrable and the bolts of electrical static had been constant, nearly violent. It was always that way when a soul is sent back into the world, they are guided through the storm level into the material plane to awaken as a newborn and begin the life cycle again.

Angelica's leaving had distracted him since that day, but it had become impossible to ignore after he'd been allowed to relive their honeymoon on Waikiki Beach.

Since then, he'd been fully distracted and unable to forget his past life.

His conflict had been noted by Orion and the council would be requesting his decision soon. A decision he was no closer to making. What he wanted to do wasn't what he felt he should do, and he had no resolution for the dilemma in his soul.

"Do you say 'Aye' Dylan or 'Nay'? The council is awaiting your response."

The deep voice of Orion drew his attention back to the present and Dylan realized, as he looked around at the others on the council, he had not heard a word of the council's summation for the guides before them. He had no idea how he should answer.

"Aye!" he consented with a less than affirmative nod but his weak response held no conviction.

Orion's gaze fixed on him with disappointment and Dylan shifted uncomfortably, there would be no more time given to him.

He *would* be asked to choose.

*   *   *

CHAPTER 6

The traffic was light for a Saturday afternoon as Jon cruised over the 59th street Bridge to the Queens Borough side.

She and Jon would be at her parent's just in time for dinner.

"Did you notice if I locked my apartment door?" Caro glanced nervously at Jon.

She hated feeling less than perfect in the simplest of things, like remembering to lock a door and yet it sometimes felt like a rebellion but against whom was she rebelling?

"Yes, Caro you did… and you even rattled the door knob twice to be sure it was locked." Jon reassured her used to her idiosyncrasy. Sometimes he'd lock her door if she did forget and he'd never tell she hadn't. He never thought it was a big deal anyway.

"Thanks," she relaxed immediately and looked out the car window.

The New York City skyline was dark and foreboding and the sky was turning that unnatural shade of green that heralds a real down pour. They'd be having a storm by the time they reached her parent's house.

"Jon? Do you think we'll make it before the first raindrop?"

"Not likely."

For someone so fond of nature in all other ways, it surprised Jon how much Caro hated a rain storm, especially if there was thunder and lightning. As if to confirm it, a brilliant bolt of lightning arrowed down from the clouds followed by a sharp crack of thunder and Caro moved closer to Jon.

Jon smiled, Caro might not like storms but he sure did!

He eased his arm around her to bring her closer as well as to comfort her.

Ten minutes later, they pulled up in front of her parent's home.

Jon pulled into the driveway but they remained in the car. The rain was pouring down and they waiting for the worst of the storm to pass.

After another ten minutes of waiting, the rain was still falling steadily but the thunder sounded farther away.

"Do you want to make a run for it?" Jon asked hugging her slightly for reassurance.

"Do you think the lightning has stopped?"

He could hear the quiver in her voice; she had a real fear of lightning.

"I counted after the last thunder clap and I think it's moved at least ten miles away," he said with total confidence in his calculation.

"All right then let's go now!" She scooted away from him and pushed open the door. She threw her coat over her head and ran quickly up the stairs of her parent's house.

She stood under the large awning over the front door waiting for Jon to join her.

Jon stepped out of the car into the rain and sprinted after her.

"Thanks Caro. I thought we were going to share your coat to keep dry," Jon shouted as he ran with no protection against the rain. He made it to the top step and shook his head like a friendly wet puppy spraying her face with water.

"Stop!" she screamed and giggled as she pushed against him.

He shook his head closer and she backed up just as the door opened.

They both fell into the foyer, nearly tumbling onto the floor at her mother's feet.

"Children, when will you two stop playing in the rain? I thought by now you'd have more sense. Look at the two of you."

Sylvia Martinelli frowned at them but her words were tempered with affection even as she shook her head at the tousled haired young man.

She liked Jonathon and wished Caro would settle down with him but her daughter had stars in her eyes, literally. She didn't understand it. It was obvious to her that Jon loved her daughter very much and Caro should have noticed it too by now.

"Here give me that wet thing," she took Caro's coat and then pointed to Jon, "And you go get a towel from the closet and dry off your hair. You'll catch a cold."

"Yes, Mother Martinelli," Jon said dutifully and kissed her cheek.

"Is that you Caro?" Nick Martinelli, Caro's dad, called out to her from his usual weekend perch in front of the TV. He was sitting in his large overstuffed recliner watching a Yankee's baseball game. "Hi, Dad," Caro walked over to him and kissed his cheek but his eyes never left the screen.

The Yankees were hosting the Red Sox, and at the moment the Red Sox were winning and her Dad was not happy.

"What kind of call was that? That was a ball not a strike you blind idiot! It was way outside and high," he stood up and gestured with his hands, "This Ump is fixing the game he must be from Boston," he huffed and sat back down in his chair as he asked Caro, "Did you see that bad call? It practically hit the on deck batter it was so far out and he calls it a strike!"

"Yes, Dad…should we have him shot?" she agreed and asked dutifully.

Her Dad chuckled and finally looked away from the screen.

"How's my best girl? Huh? Are you enjoying that new job?"

"I love it. I think I'm dreaming when I'm there. It's just too much fun to be called work and too good to be true."

"That's what it's like when you actually pursue something you enjoy in life," he chucked her under the chin, "a lot different than taking a job just to pay the bills. I'm glad it worked out for you Caro. Is Jon with you?"

"Yes, but Mom sent him to dry off. He got wet out in the rain with me."

"What?" He asked but his eyes were focused again on the game.

Caro smiled and sat down on the arm of his chair to watch the baseball drama.

The pitch was in and the ump called a ball.

Her father was in a trance now. The count was full at three balls and two strikes. The next pitch was critical since the Yanks were down 4 runs to 2 and it was the bottom of the ninth.

The pitch was inside and the batter slammed it back across the field, up and into the stands for a home run.

"Yeah, that's the way to do it! Don't give 'um another chance to make a bad call send it out of the park baby!" Nick stood up and shouted.

It was a wonder to Caro that the neighbors hadn't complained over the years. Her father was such an avid baseball fan and loudly enthusiastic about it, she was sure you could hear him a block away.

Since his beloved Yankees now had a chance to win he relaxed back in his chair.

"Can I bring anything in for you Dad? Would you like something to drink?"

He turned and smiled at her, "That would be nice, mia Caro, and tell that boyfriend of yours to get in here he's going to miss the play of the century. I can feel it."

"Sure Dad, I'll send Jon in."

She loved the way her Dad called her 'mia Caro'. It was an endearment he'd used for her since she was very little and it always made her feel loved.

Caro brought two beers in for her Dad and Jon who had joined him in the family room. The game was in extra innings as the Yankees had tied it up in the ninth.

"Mom said dinner would be ready in about fifteen minutes," she placed the beers on the coffee table in front of them but neither seemed to hear her.

"Dad, did you hear me?"

"Okay," he mumbled as he reached for his beer.

Jon winked at her and took a long pull on his beer, too content to answer.

Caro shook her head and went back to her mom in the kitchen.

"Did you tell them dear?" her mom asked as she checked the roast in the oven.

"I told them but if they heard me, well that's a different question."

Caro sat down on the stool by the kitchen counter.

"If the game continues we'll just have to serve them in front of the television set. You know your dad and Baseball Season, everything else is on autopilot, especially during a Yankee game."

"I know," Caro laughed and picked off a piece of crust from a cooling apple pie on the counter. "Oh, I meant to ask if you kept my old telescope. The one I had in my room."

"Yes, I think it's one of the things your dad and I had stored away when you went to college. Why dear? Did you need it now?"

"I'd like to give it to this little boy, Michael. He was one of the children in my first school group and he's been by the museum twice this week with his older brother. I think he has a genuine interest in Astronomy and I think he'd appreciate it."

"That's very kind of you. You might find it in one of the boxes in your closet but ask your dad he might have put it away in the attic."

"I'll ask him after we eat."

The timer on the oven went off and her mom sighed, "The roast is done. I guess it's decided then, we'll be serving them in front of the television."

"I guess so," Caro agreed and broke off another piece of the pie crust when her mom turned away to take the roast out of the oven, "I'll get the TV trays ready."

Caro had just opened the first tray when her Dad and Jon joined them in the kitchen.

"Can we help?" Jon asked.

"No, we were ready to bring this out to you."

"No need to now, the Yankees won. We can eat in the dining room."

Her father said as he pulled a piece of crust from the still cooling apple pie on the counter.

"Ah, we can dine like civilized folks and for a while I can have your undivided attention," Sylvia smiled at her husband who laughed and kissed her cheek with affection.

"You bet. I'm all yours," he looked at his watch then added, "Until five anyway…then the Mets are on."

Sylvia nudged him good naturedly and handed him the roast to bring to the table.

When they sat down Caro asked her father if he remembered packing away her telescope in a box and if it might be in her old room.

"I'm not sure but I'll help you look for it after dinner," he said as he took a forkful of the succulent roast and saluted his wife with it, "This looks great hon."

The meal was delicious and everyone attested to it with heavenly sighs and second platefuls. After desert and coffee Caro and her dad went up to her old room to find her telescope and Jon stayed to help her mom clear the dishes.

Caro searched through boxes her dad handed her from the closet and he rummaged through more boxes still stacked in the corner of her bedroom's walk in closet.

Caro thought she heard him saying something but his voice was muffled and she couldn't make out what he'd said.

"What Dad?"

"I don't think it's in here Caro. I think I may have…" he walked out from the closet as he spoke and nearly bumped into Jon who was entering her room.

"Sorry Jon," he said and sidestepped around him just in time.

"You were saying…you may have what Dad?" Caro prompted him hoping he remembered where her telescope was.

"I may have stored it in the boxes I put up in the attic. It's possible the telescope is up there."

"I'll go up and check with Caro," Jon volunteered.

"Well…I am missing the Mets game," Nick admitted and turned to Caro, "Would you mind?"

"No, of course not Dad," she smiled at him, "go watch the game. Jon can help me find it, if it's up there."

"I'm sure it is, just not certain which box it's in but you're right, Jon can help you find it."

"I'll do my best."

"Thanks," Nick smiled and slapped Jon on the back before he headed downstairs.

"Well, come on then, let's start." Caro pulled on Jon's sleeve.

"Lead the way."

Caro laughed and pushed him out into the hall.

They opened the creaking door that led up to the attic and Jon was hit full force by memories he had of special moments spent in that attic.

At Caro's tenth birthday party he and Caro had hidden behind the old furniture stored away during a game of hide and seek. He hadn't wanted to be found that day; he'd loved having her all to himself. They'd laughed at the scary shadows the darkness created from ordinary objects and enjoyed their hiding place until they were found.

That memory had been childish fun but it wasn't the only memory he'd had of Caro and that attic...and that second memory was the one tormenting him with vivid clarity.

It was a day when they were a few years older...and a bit more curious.

It was Caro's sixteenth birthday party and they'd gone up there on a dare to experiment with kissing. He remembered how his heart had nearly stopped when their lips met and how warm and soft her lips were beneath his and the thought of that kiss, even ten years later, in memory, affected him exactly the same way.

Jon was one step behind her on the stairs and looked at her walking up ahead of him.

"Caro, do you remember when we played seven minutes in heaven up here?"

Caro missed a step and nearly fell backwards. Jon's hand at her back steadied her as she stepped onto the landing before turning around to face him.

"What made you remember that?" She asked as her shocked eyes searched his.

"Remember it?"

He took the last step up to stand before her, "Caro, I don't think I've ever forgotten it," he whispered as he lowered his lips to hers and something sharp, electric, and indefinable pulled them closer together.

*　　　　　*　　　　　*

(Council on High's chamber)

Dylan felt the sharp cut of jealousy as he watched the embrace.

He shouldn't have felt it; he understood Angelica was going to experience this new life without him, experience love without him, so he shouldn't have felt the sharp edge of jealousy that sliced through his spirit...and he shouldn't have wanted to punch out the man holding her…and he really shouldn't have asked to see how she was doing.

"What is your answer Dylan?"

Orion's voice cut through his jumbled, angry thoughts. The Council wanted his decision now but he had no quick answer to give.

He couldn't look away from the frozen image before him, Angelica in that man's arms, leaning in to kiss him.

He wanted to look away, he wanted to ignore the feelings but seeing Angelica in another man's arms was not easy to ignore…and even more difficult to accept.

It mattered to him. It mattered very much…even if it shouldn't.

"Dylan can you accept she has to grow in all of life's experiences and most especially in love to attain perfection?"

Orion's kind voice cut into Dylan's thoughts and he nodded robotically but silently he answered, "Did she?"

"Dylan, you must decide your path, if it is to continue here or begin again there," Orion pointed to the image.

Dylan knew Orion had heard his thoughts and he looked away from the image. Finally, it evaporated into colored crystals of light but what it had made him feel wasn't going anywhere. Was it too late to be a part of her new life?

"Dylan, you must know that if you go back, she could love you or reject you," Orion warned him, "It is not predetermined that you will spend this lifetime together."

Dylan gave him an annoyed look. If Orion were going to continue to read his thoughts he may as well just speak them out loud.

"I understand that but if I go back our paths *will* cross." Dylan's voice was strong and sure now. Maybe he had already decided.

"Yes, that is inevitable, souls will find ways to reconnect to those they love but it is not inevitable that it will matter."

Dylan thought it would matter very much and he believed what he and Angelica had once shared would transcend even a new life path and overshadow this new love she was contemplating. He did believe if he went back, it would be as it once was between them.

Orion tried to instill reality and said with what sounded like fatherly concern, "There will be no memory of your past with Angelica, for her or *you*, once you cross over you'll retain no memory of this existence or your past life."

"I understand."

Orion sighed, "Then it is time to speak your decision," he nodded to the mists of storm clouds hovering over the council awaiting that decision.

Dylan looked towards the encroaching storm and his eyes widened.

It was the passage way to life, the way he had guided many through, including Angelica. He'd coached younger guardians on how to navigate the storm and deliver the soul back into the life cycle and he'd always walked through it fearlessly but suddenly, he wondered if he could. Could he completely give up everything? For the first time, he had true empathy for those souls who had returned to life.

"I -" Dylan began but before he could give his answer, David, interrupted him.

"Dylan before you decide, I can tell you I have spoken to Angelica and she is acclimating very well to her new life."

61

"So I've seen," Dylan's tone was dry with sarcasm, a human tone he had not used or felt since coming into this level of existence, and it gave him pause but that image of her kissing another was not going away. He didn't want to hear David's summation, he'd already decided. He turned to Orion.

"What shall it be?" Orion asked quietly.

Dylan answered without hesitation feeling more human than spirit as the heartbeat grew strong within him; it was time to reclaim his love.

CHAPTER 7

"Black holes which had until rather recently been unknown to us are now being discovered almost daily in our universe…" The click of the computer keys as she frantically typed out the words coming over her headset was rhythmical.

Caro had not attended last nights meeting but this morning she was given the recorded transcript to type and add to the large volume of written records that were kept in the office.

The meeting was interesting and filled with so much fascinating information she had to play back some lines several times before she typed them. She was engrossed in every word as she listened and typed. Oblivious to everything around her she nearly jumped out of her chair when someone touched her shoulder.

She looked up startled to see Professor Noah D. Bradley smiling down at her.

"Yes sir?" she took off her headphones and turned to him.

"You work too hard Caroline. I wanted to let you know it's nearly two p.m. and you haven't taken a lunch yet."

Caro smiled cautiously. She didn't know Professor Bradley very well. He'd started working with the team of astrophysicists only a week ago but he'd searched her out several times this week to ask her for notes on prior research meetings.

"I guess I lost track of the time. I'll finish this last speaker and I'll break for lunch," she started to put her headphones back on but his hand touched hers to stop the motion.

"I haven't had lunch either and wondered if you'd join me at the café. We could share a table."

Caro felt the warm hand on hers and looked up into his dark, very interested in her answer, green eyes but she certainly didn't want to encourage anything with Mr. Bradley. Her heart was with Jon and she wasn't even a little bit tempted to give Professor, admittedly very good looking, Bradley here a chance to change that.

She shook her head, "I'm not sure that would be a good id-"

"I understand," he cut her off before she could finish refusing him and lifted his hand from hers.

"I…" she started to apologize but stopped herself. She didn't need to apologize but it didn't matter because he'd already turned his back and retreated to his office across the hall. She'd stared at his broad shouldered frame as he walked away.

He was handsome, very handsome, and when they were first introduced his beautiful eyes had struck a chord of recognition in her, a feeling that made her more than a little uncomfortable around him.

Caro put the headphones down and picked up the phone; she punched in the number she knew by heart and waited a moment before it was picked up on the other   end.

"Hi! What are you doing?" she asked in a low voice.

"Talking to a beautiful woman at the moment and wondering why she's calling?"

The tenderness in Jon's voice flowed over the phone wires and it was just what she needed to rid herself of the uncomfortable feelings the new professor had caused.

She smiled easily as she answered, "She called because she's missing a very handsome someone and wondering if he could meet her for lunch?" She wanted him here, close enough to calm the sudden, inexplicable fear she had of losing what they had just found.

"I wish I could Caro, I really do but right now, I've got a deadline and I'm pressing it," he said regretfully, looking down at the half finished comic strip on his board and fighting back the urge to forget his work and go to her, "Can I coax you to forgive me if I make you dinner here tonight, grilled steaks and salad and a promise to offer you food, wine, candle light and my undivided attention."

"Sure, and of course I understand," she agreed easily but disappointment was evident in her voice. She scolded her self for it. She didn't need to have Jon in front of her to remember that what they were discovering about their feelings was everything to her. She was just being silly, letting another man's obvious interest in her shake her up, and even sillier to think there was some odd moment of recognition between them when he was a complete stranger to her.

She cupped her hand over the phone and whispered in a husky voice, "I'll bring the wine and the warm bread from the bakery and meet you in your apartment by six."

"Never mind the warm bread just bring your warm self," Jon's voice turned husky with longing as his concentration solely centered on her, the comic strip would take a little longer to finish now.

Caro smiled and whispered, "I'll be there. Bye Jon."

"Bye, love."

The line went silent and she cradled the phone another minute before she hung up.

May as well go to lunch now, she decided and disconnected her headset.

She closed the computer, and grabbed her purse. Taking one quick look to see that Professor Bradley was not in the hall she hurried past his office and on to the café.

Noah walked into the café and noticed Caroline sitting alone at a table, reading a magazine and sipping a coffee. He took a seat at a table in the back of the café away from her but he couldn't stop looking at her.

After she'd rejected his invitation he'd gone back to his office but decided to try again to convince her to have lunch with him. When he'd walked back to her office he hadn't intended to over hear her private conversation, but he had. It was obviously someone she cared about or possibly married to. Maybe she didn't wear a ring but the bottom line; she was very serious about the person on the other end of that phone call.

It shouldn't bother him, he didn't even know her…so why *did* it bother him?

They'd only just met but the moment he'd seen her, looked into her eyes, something deep inside of him acknowledged her. What it was he couldn't say but he thought she'd felt it too.

Now he had to come to terms with the fact that she was in a relationship and he'd have to ignore whatever this attraction was.

The waitress stopped at his table and drew his attention away from Caroline.

"Would you like to order?"

"Just some coffee," he replied with a smile.

The waitress nodded and walked away.

Noah watched the waitress make her way to Caroline's table. He watched as they conversed and it appeared they were friends.

"Can you feel the fire on the back of your head?" Nancy refilled Caro's cup and asked her in a whisper as she glanced back at the gorgeous blond haired, green-eyed hunk that had been in the Café a few times this last week.

"What?" Caro looked up from her magazine.

"The new guy in the Astro-pack," as she liked to call the group of physicists at the museum, "He's staring at you like you're a gourmet meal and he's been starving for a while."

Caro shifted in her seat, the analogy felt apropos for the way he'd made her feel earlier. "I know... he's interested but I'm definitely not. Jon and I are just starting to work out this new relationship of being more than best friends and I love Jon."

Nancy nodded kindly, "Then what ever you do don't turn around. Pay your bill and run, don't walk, to the elevators," she placed Caro's check on the table and looked over her shoulder at the very handsome six-foot plus form of masculine perfection staring unwaveringly at Caro.

She bent down again and whispered. "And Good luck!"

*   *   *

Caro watched Jon flip the steaks on the small grill out on his terrace. She walked around his living room picking things up and putting them back down. She loved his apartment. The walls were painted a soft sable and the molded wood on each wall was painted a rich cream color accenting the warmth of the room. The furniture was invitingly comfortable from the two large over-stuffed couches that faced each other to the well-worn lounger in the corner. His work area, a slanted drawing board set up in front of a heavily padded barstool was strewn with his drawings of the little tykes 'Cal and Ivy'.

She long suspected they were images of her and Jon as children because many of the strips hit home with their humor and many stirred memories too true to forget.

She smiled as she moved the boards and looked at his current work in progress.

Little Ivy was trying to learn how to play baseball to impress the new boy in town. Her best friend Cal was trying to help her but it was useless. She couldn't hit the ball even if it was the size of a basketball, and finally that's just what he throws at her.

Caro laughed at the humor but then had a sobering thought.

Maybe Jon was a little too insightful. The new kid in town was giving her a problem but she certainly didn't want to make him notice her.

She walked away from the cartoon but couldn't shake the uneasy feeling that had been with her since she left the café.

Just knowing that Noah had watched her the whole time made her feel strange and she wanted to come home and talk to Jon about it but she realized that had changed.

She couldn't tell him everything anymore. This new road they were on had a few pot holes she hadn't seen. She sighed deeply.

"Steaks will be done in a minute," Jon said from the open terrace door.

"I'm fine. I had a late lunch," she walked back to the table. He'd set it up for a romantic dinner, candle light and all. She smiled and sat down.

"Was it that busy today?" he checked the vegetables grilling on the side and then turned his attention fully on her.

"No. Not really, I just took a late lunch," she said and toyed with her wine glass moving it in circles on the tablecloth.

Jon watched her closely, knowing every nuance of her personality he knew she was worrying over something.

"Was it a bad day?"

"Huh?"

She glanced up quickly nearly spilling the wine, "No, not really."

"Something happen that upset you?" he asked casually as he brought the finished steaks over to the table along with the side of grilled vegetables.

"No," she said with a laugh but it fell flat. She knew Jon could see right through her attempt to sound casual but how *could* she tell him what was bothering her? And how could she not. Jon was staring at her with a raised brow waiting for the truth just as he had hundreds of times before, over the many years of their friendship; he *knew* when she was holding back her feelings.

"Fine…but it's no big deal."

"Tell me anyway."

"Okay…there's this new guy at work and…well…he makes me a little uncomfortable."

"Why?" His tone mildly curious but his senses went on alert. He wondered if that new guy was the reason she'd called him unexpectedly this afternoon to meet her for lunch? Now he wished he had.

"I don't know why…there's no reason really."

"There must be something." Jon's eyes searched hers.

"I just find him hanging around the office too much."

"He hangs around you?"

"No, nothing like that, he isn't stalking me," she laughed nervously and shook her head but maybe it did feel a little like stalking when they were in the cafe. Should she tell him about lunch? No, she was being overly sensitive to a little attention. Tomorrow he probably wouldn't even talk to her. She hoped.

"Then what is it about him that makes you uncomfortable?"

"It's silly…He just interrupts my work requesting data. He's a bit of a pain that's all," she said firmly and pulled her plate closer, "This looks great Jon."

She jabbed a fork full of vegetables and began eating heartily.

Maybe he'd imagined the nervousness, maybe he was too sensitive to the fragility of their new relationship…maybe…but he didn't think so. Whatever it was about this new guy at work, she wasn't telling him everything.

"Some wine?" he asked and she nodded eagerly. Yes, he could see it in her eyes; she was uncomfortable about something and avoiding telling him.

He poured more wine into her glass and then topped off his.

It was an unusual situation to be in with Caro because they'd always told each other everything. Taking baby steps with their feelings this way and avoiding the truth was new territory for them but every new relationship had to have an adjustment period. He hadn't thought they would need one but if they had to have a few weeks of wobble it certainly wasn't anything he couldn't handle, because he intended to share forever with her, and a few uncomfortable first weeks was nothing compared to that.

"That was an excellent steak Jon. You're spoiling me."

His arms were around her and she was snuggled back against him on the couch.

"That was my intention," he admitted hugging her closer.

"It worked," she said softly, and it had. She was no longer worried about the unwanted attention from a stranger at work. She was only aware of Jon as she had been since day one of kindergarten. He was her constant and what he didn't know was that in sixth grade she'd secretively been attracted to him but there was always a new girl getting in the way of her telling him back then and then they grew up and stayed close but never intimate and friendship just seemed the easiest way to be around him, until that kiss on her attic steps three weeks ago.

A cool breeze blew in from the open terrace door and she breathed in the crispness of it.

"I love your apartment. You get the night breezes on this side of the building. I never get any stirring of air in my rooms at night."

71

"Then you should spend your nights here and enjoy the night's magic with me," he whispered in her ear.

Caro turned in his arms, his eyes were intensely dark and their chocolaty richness was melting her. He was incredibly handsome but she wasn't ready yet to take the final step, to become lovers, to move into commitment territory, not before she knew for sure she could take that step. Not before she knew, she no longer feared it.

But fear or not her mind and body were curious enough and seriously considering his question. This was the first time Jon had actually asked her to stay over…what would it be like…to be held in his arms…all night…

"Stay here tonight," he whispered then lowered his lips to hers and kissed her.

The kiss moved them easily down into the rich, sensual softness of the couch.

"Will you stay?"

His lips a fraction away from hers waited for her answer.

Her lips moved and his attention was laser focused as they formed a word that appeared to begin with a y. Then his heart sank in frustration as the phone jangled loudly breaking the moment.

"Ignore it," he demanded but already knew she couldn't.

"Jon you have to answer it."

It was another Caro quirk; she'd worry if she missed a ringing phone, worry they'd leave no message, or they'd called from a number she didn't have in her contacts. She'd think how it may have been important and her concern extended to any friend's unanswered phone call too, fearing a missed opportunity or a dire circumstance that could have been avoided.

"They'll leave a message," frustration evident in his tone.

"They might not and it could be important."

Jon sighed heavily, "Promise you won't move," he compelled her with a searing look and she nodded.

Still he hesitated a second longer hoping the caller would hang up but the phone was on its third ring and it didn't seem like the caller was going to give up, and stupidly he'd set his message to answer on five rings.

Who does that? He grumbled silently. He was changing it tomorrow to two…maybe even one. He decided as he walked towards the offending device.

"Hello!"

He barked harshly into the receiver but a second later his expression turned regretful.

"Hi Mom, no, you aren't interrupting anything."

He looked heavenward hoping his small lie would pass.

"I was just finishing dinner and Caro's here…No; I guess she didn't have a date tonight." He smiled at Caro and watched as she snuggled deeper into the couch making him wish he were next to her. He gripped the phone tighter closing his eyes and tuning out his mom's voice for a brief moment.

"What? Sorry, I didn't hear you…Oh sure, I remember. Yes, I'll be going," he sighed but then smiled widely, "Absolutely, yes, I'm *sure* Caro would love to come with me to Ben's wedding," he grinned wickedly as he watched her sit up and become totally interest in his conversation.

Ben was his cousin. Younger by one year but had always tried to outdo his older cousin in everything. He and Ben didn't always get along but they were family and so he had to go to the wedding, whether he wanted to or not but now he suddenly did, since Caro *would* be going with him.

"Yes, I'll tell her you said hello," he winked at Caro and nearly dropped the phone when she smiled invitingly back at him and hugged a throw pillow to her chest.

"Uh, yeah...Love you too...Bye," he quickly ended the call.

Caro watched as he tried to hang up the phone. It appeared his hands were suddenly unable to coordinate the simple command. Finally, he got it to stay in the cradle and he walked back to her.

His eyes shone with intent and there was determination in his stride.

Caro smiled at him as her heart rate increased. There was no way to deny the attraction between them tonight.

"Ben's wedding? When did that happen?" she asked when he sat down and pulled her back into his arms.

"Last year, he met his future wife while on vacation in France. It turned out she lived only ten miles from him in New Jersey." He answered but his eyes telegraphed a whole other meaning, not at all connected to his mundane accounting of his cousin's love life.

"And now he's getting married." Caro's eyes smiled into his.

"Yes, he's told everyone it was love at first sight," Jon's eyes roamed her face lovingly, giving his words his own meaning.

"Imagine that, little Ben finding love at first sight and getting married," she said as she held his gaze.

"Yeah, Ben's getting married," he said then murmured softly, "Lucky Ben."

Jon's eyes darkened and for the first time in his life he truly envied his cousin. He wanted nothing more than to be getting married, and to no one else but Caro.

Caro's heart sped up when she'd heard the way he caressed the word 'married'. Her gaze sharpened but it was no longer clouded with desire it was slightly tinged with fear. Her stomach clenched at the thought of commitment and it had nothing to do with Jon. She had no idea why this ridiculous fear was a part of her or why it would still rear its head with Jon. She loved him enough to really think about forever with him but right now her fear of that forever was still too alive for her to hope it would go away tonight, even for him, but why?

An image of Noah Bradley suddenly rose in her mind and she shook it quickly way. Why would she think of him at this moment? The unwanted image had further shaken her confidence.

"Caro," Jon whispered, "I believe, before I answered that phone call, you were going to answer my question."

His smile was easy but his eyes were dangerously serious.

Caro still felt the desire to stay with him but that uncalled for image of Noah and her fear won out. She looked away.

"I can't Jon, not tonight…I should go."

She was upset with herself. Her indecision and her inexplicable fear would hurt them both if she didn't get a handle on it and why in all that was messed up enough already was she thinking of a total stranger at a moment of intimacy with Jon?

That question and its possible answers concerned her even more.

Jon stood up and held his hand out to her, "Come on, I'll walk you home."

His look reassured her he was fine with her decision, his thick golden brown hair fell across his brow and she was lost in the tenderness of his loving eyes.

How could she not pull him back down and take the night back to where it was going? How could she leave him standing there tall and strong with his hand out to her in support of her stupid reactions?

She breathed deeply, but her stupid reactions were not going away even if she knew they were stupid. So instead of pulling him back down into the softness of the couch she took his hand and stood up too.

He tugged on her hand and smiled, "We've got a lot more between us then one derailed night."

"I know."

And she did. He was Jon, her best friend and he understood her completely, like no one else ever had, or ever would and he loved her. What more could she ask for? When another unwanted image of Noah flashed in her mind her heart squeezed with sharp concern. What the hell was wrong with her?

Jon walked her across the hall and stopped at her door.

"I love you Caro, I'll see you tomorrow."

He kissed her gently but she was desperate to ignore what was happening to her so she pulled him closer and kissed him harder.

"I love you Jon," she whispered reverently against his lips, "Don't ever doubt that."

"I never would," he promised before deepening the kiss.

Caro lost herself in the feel of his arms holding her, needing to make him her only reality before going into her lonely apartment where it was going to be a very long night of a one sided conversation.

CHAPTER 8

Caro ushered the group of third-graders through the cosmic pathway. The children were wide eyed and focused on her every word.

She had grown into her position as tour guide, and had learned just how to modulate her voice for effect and loved the children's reactions to her descriptions of space, time and the universe.

When she showed them the 15-ton meteorite in the Hall of the Universe their little mouths dropped open.

"This fell from space?" one little boy asked as he gaped at the enormity of the object.

All the children listened intently for her answer.

"Yes it did," she said solemnly, trying not to smile, "thousands of years ago."

"Is this the one that took out the dinosaurs?" asked one little girl, curiosity shinning in her big, brown eyes.

"No, but then again...maybe it's like the one that did," she whispered and couldn't contain a smile as she watched the children reach out to touch the surface, amazed that it had fallen from the sky and could possible be like the thing that killed all the dinosaurs. You could almost see their imaginations soaring with possibilities.

Caro loved their wonder, their sense of adventure, just being with them renewed her belief in the human race.

After all, they were the next generation and if they could keep that focus, that simple desire to learn and imagine there would be no limits to the world they could create, or the bold new worlds they'd be discovering when they became adults.

"Let's move on to the next exhibit," she said but it took some coaxing before they would leave the meteorite to walk over to the aquatic ecosystem contained in a large round glass.

After they marveled at the watery universe she lined them up to take turns stepping on the scales imbedded in the museum's floor so they could see their weight on other planets.

The teachers took over for the tour through the Hall of Planet Earth.

The children were placed into small groups and each group was given a search and discover map. They had to follow the map of the room, discover all the facts it outlined and answer several questions.

Apparently, there was a competition to be the first to finish.

Caro stood back watching the children quickly trying to find the answers to the questions on their papers.

"Nice group of kids."

The deep voice behind her was close and becoming too familiar. He hadn't spoken to her in the last week and she'd hoped his interest in her had faded, just as she'd hoped the unexplainable images of him would stop forming in her mind.

She turned around and faced him.

"Hello, Mr. Bradley, taking a tour of the museum today?"

"No, but I caught your explanation of the expanding universe and hung on your every word. I had to follow your tour...You're a very good guide."

"Thank you," she turned away because her cheeks were turning pink. The compliment made her feel good but something about his closeness had affected her too. Something in her was feeling attracted to him, and she didn't like it one bit.

She injected coolness into her next words, "I can't see how my knowledge could fascinate such a learned professor, but I thank you for the compliment."

He stepped closer, "You shouldn't sell yourself short Caroline. Your fascination with the universe is what makes your telling of it so interesting. Your voice captures and your rich descriptions feed the imagination. You're the perfect guide for these young minds. You help them discover."

His sincerity vibrated through her and she turned back to him.

"I do love guiding them but I can't believe you can see that."

"I can see a lot of things...like the way you avoid me and the fact that you're not unaffected by our chemistry."

His beautiful green eyes studied her face as he spoke.

"I...I have a boyfriend," she said lamely and knew it sounded unconvincing but those eyes shook her confidence and reached into her soul drawing a recognition she didn't understand and didn't want.

"I know," he said it simply.

Uneasy with the pull of attraction she told him, "I have to catch up to my tour now," and quickly walked away crossing the room and pausing to speak with one of the teachers. It was cowardly but she couldn't help it. Something was happening between them that she didn't understand and wanted even less.

Noah watched her walk away. He waited for her to look back at him, give him some sign she acknowledge the attraction between them, but she didn't. She was casually conversing with the young schoolteacher across the room while he stood there like a love starved fool, watching her, waiting for a morsel of her attention and he didn't know why he didn't leave.

Yesterday, he'd been offered a position with Princeton University. Maybe he should accept the position, and forget about her.

That's exactly what he should do, his mind acknowledged the decision, but his body didn't move. He stood there as she gathered the children and walked them out of the hall.

She never looked back once.

What more proof did he need? Why pursue her? She had a boyfriend, she'd told him so, though not a husband...still... she'd made her position clear. He would stop trying to catch her attention, he should forget about her.

He turned and walked back to his office while seriously considering the offer from Princeton.

*   *   *

It was Friday. Caro had made it through the rest of the week without any other unsettling encounters with Noah Bradley. She was relieved the week was over and now she could look forward to the weekend.

This Saturday she and Jon were driving to New Jersey for Ben's wedding.

She looked at her desk clock, it was after five, past time to go home and get the weekend started.

She locked her desk, shut off her computer and grabbed her purse and coat. When she snapped off the office light she noticed the rain falling heavily just outside her window so she went back and took her emergency umbrella out of her bottom desk drawer.

Caro stepped outside into the pouring rain and opened her umbrella. The street lights shimmered in the puddles as she walked along the sidewalk to the edge of curb.

Usually she took the train home but today she'd decided to treat herself to a cab ride.

She raised her hand as she spied several yellow taxis coming down the street but she didn't see the man under a large umbrella standing close behind her who was also signaling for a ride.

The yellow cab that answered her summons splattered her with water as it pulled up sharply to the curb.

Caro jumped back immediately colliding with someone behind her and nearly lost her footing but a strong arm wrapped around her to steady her just as her umbrella flew sideways revealing her rescuer.

Caro found herself held tightly in Noah Bradley's arms, staring up into his darkly lashed emerald eyes. She was frozen for a moment in the unplanned embrace before she apologized and stepped away.

Noah stepped back without a word and signaled for another cab. Immediately one pulled in behind the first and he turned and headed over to it.

The window on the cab in front of Caro automatically rolled down.

"Sorry, I got ya' wet lady!" the driver leaned over and yelled out the passenger window to her. "Where ya' headed?"

Caro was held in a surreal feeling of déjà vu as she watched Noah get into his cab. When it drove by her she saw he was watching her just as intently.

"Hey do you want a ride somewhere or not?" The cab driver yelled his question to her.

In an almost trance like state Caro nodded and got into the back seat of the cab.

Her heart was not pounding she scolded herself, and if it was it was not pounding because of his brief but warm embrace or his unwavering stare…and mostly not because of how familiar it felt to be in his arms. She was definitely not attracted to him.

"I love Jon, I'm in love with Jon," she murmured over and over during the long ride home. He was her lifeline and she would not lose him over a crazy and very unwanted attraction.

*   *   *

The room was dark but for the small glow from a street lamp just beyond his window.

Noah watched the rain splatter against the window pane, his eyes following the stray drops as they zigzagged down the window's glass.

He hadn't found sleep tonight. He'd tossed and turned most of the night, finally deciding he'd had enough of trying to fight it.

Now he was staring out at the bleakness beyond his window, waiting for the dawn and wondering why she mattered to him. He knew very little about her and she didn't seem intent on allowing him to get any closer to change that.

He was not a pain junkie. He would get over whatever pull he felt for her and he had a whole weekend to straighten out this foolish allure, a whole weekend to forget she exists, a whole weekend to forget how she felt against him in the rain and how he knew if he'd kissed her…her kiss would be maddeningly sweet and passionate. How he knew that was a mystery but he had a whole weekend to get over it…and her.

CHAPTER 9

Caro and Jon drove through the countryside, on their way to Ben's wedding.

The cool, late October breeze stirred the colors in the trees and shook the beautiful red and orange leaves down to the ground.

She loved autumn, especially when the leaves changed. She thought nature at its most artistic when it painted New York in blazing color just before turning it into the stark white of winter. She simply loved autumn. It made her feel so alive. She rolled down the window to let the crisp, fresh October air into the car.

"Hey! You're freezing the driver here."

"Nonsense Jon it feels great, keeps the blood flowing."

"Not mine. It's solidifying as we speak," he grumbled good-naturedly.

"It's only fifty degrees outside you won't freeze," she laughed at his huddled position over the wheel and rolled the window back up, leaving just a small crack to let the cool air in.

"You can keep the window open if you can find a way to keep the driver warm," he challenged in a low voice.

Caro studied his profile, chiseled handsomeness and strength, and his full face was just as arresting.

Caro slid closer to him but when she moved to put her hand on his arm she felt suddenly awkward and stopped at the same moment he turned to her and noticed her hesitation.

For a brief instant, before he turned his attention back to the traffic, she'd seen the desire in his eyes and felt warmed by it. Maybe this weekend they would cross that threshold, figuratively and intimately.

They drove a few more miles before they pulled into the parking lot of Saint Joseph's Roman Catholic Church.

Jon's Parents waited for them near the church's entrance.

"Do we let them know we're a couple?" Jon asked when they got out of the car.

"Let's start as friends and see when the moment feels right to tell them," Caro said as they walked towards the church to join them.

The ceremony was solemn and beautiful.

Caro felt a stirring of unwanted and mixed emotions as the couple pledged their love. Would she ever be able to make those vows? Only if she could get over her total fear of commitment and since she had no clue why she feared it, she'd no clue how to conquer it but if she could, she glanced at Jon and smiled, she'd definitely vow to share forever with him.

The Reception hall was near the church and after the ceremony they walked over to the elegant ballroom. It was filled to capacity with a couple hundred wedding guests.

Jon and his cousin Ben shared a very large family and more than half the guests there were relatives of the groom.

Caro walked up to the rolling bar and requested a white wine.

The waiter had filled the glass nearly to the brim and she almost spilled it on Jon's expensively well-tailored jacket when she turned around.

"Jon! I didn't know you were standing so close behind me."

"It's not nearly as close as I'd like to be love," he whispered as he stilled the glass in her hand and used the movement as an excuse to pull her closer.

"You want to *tell* your parents we're dating or do you just want to *show* them?" she whispered saucily.

"Oh, I think they'll figure it out by themselves," he put his arms around her waist and pulled her even closer as she balanced her drink precariously in her hand.

"Yeah, their definitely going to suspect something," she smiled warmly up at him.

Anyone with eyes could see they were more than friends.

"Hey guys take it to the garden. You're stopping the flow of liquor here."

The voice behind them was good-natured and familiar.

"Congratulations Ben," Jon said as he turned to his cousin but still held Caro close to his side.

"Can I soon say the same to you?" Ben's eyebrows lifted as he looked Caro up and down and shook Jon's hand.

"You don't remember Caroline Martinelli?"

"Caroline?" Ben stood back and looked her over again. "Wow, I really didn't recognize you but then it has been years since grade school and I was the grade behind you guys."

"It's all right. I'm not sure I'd have recognized you either, Ben," she smiled back at him looking him up and down as he had done to her and making him laugh.

"So...have you two been dating long? 'Cause Aunt Jane never said a word to anyone about it and I would have thought—"

"No!" They answered in unison but then Jon continued in a quieter tone.

"No, we haven't been dating long and we haven't exactly let my parent's know."

"Got it," Ben winked at Jon and turned to Caro, "Our family is big on weddings. They can't get enough of them, as you can see by the multitudes of relatives here. We just keep multiplying." He laughed at his own wit and then pointed out a young couple standing near the bride.

"See Michael and Jessie over there near my lovely wife Annette? We're going to their wedding next month. Michael is twenty-five and he's the oldest of Aunt Abigail and Uncle Frank's sons. Their middle son is James he's standing with his wife Maggie, the beauty in the blue dress," he pointed out another young couple standing across the room. "They've been married for nearly two years and have one year old twin sons. And over there," he took Caro by the shoulders and turned her around to look at the other side of the room where he pointed out two more people, "Mary and Jennifer, Aunt Sophia's daughters. Mary has three children and the fourth is, as you can see, well on the way. Jennifer has five boys and at the relief of her husband Doug has given up on trying for the girl...and...do you see the tall blond haired man standing next to Jennifer?"

Caro nodded.

"That's my older brother Zach, he and his wife Emily have two little girls. I'm sure you're beginning to see the pattern here...right?" He asked and turned her back to face him but she didn't answer she just stared at him.

He laughed as he enlightened her.

"Every Forbes is happily married with elaborate weddings captured in photographs in their family albums attesting to the family's love for celebration," he leaned closer to her and whispered sagely, "My Dad and our Aunts Sophie, Margaret and Abigail all have big families, big celebrations. Uncle Paul, Jon's father..." he shook his head sadly at Jon then whispered in her ear, "Jon here is an '*only*'," he stressed the word, "while everyone else has tons of siblings, he's been on his own. So you can see...any inkling on the wind of a relationship turning serious for Jon-boy here and...Boom!" He clapped his hand for effect and Caro jumped, "They've got your hall set up and the church date written in the parish register," he laughed at the stunned expression on Caro's face and slapped Jon on the back. "It won't be long before I'll be attending your wedding right Jon-boy?"

Jon would have loved to deck his cousin but it wouldn't have been proper and Ben just thought he was being witty. So instead, Jon stared back at him with a wry smile because Ben never changed, he always loved to set a stage and shake things up.

Caro stared wide-eyed at Ben and wondering, would they really push her and Jon to get engaged? Yes, of course they would. She hadn't thought of that. She loved Jon's family very much. They were like a second set of parents to her and they had always treated her like family but if they knew...would everything change?

Jon saw the revelations in her eyes and didn't want her to go there. Nothing was going to ruin tonight. Luckily, the band began to play a slow song and it felt like a cue.

"Come on Caro, let's dance," he put his arm around her and led her away from Ben.

"I hope you don't mind," he looked back at his cousin.

"Not me. I'm a happy man tonight. I think everyone should be in love," Ben smiled and then turned to the waiter and ordered the drink he had walked over for ten minutes ago.

Caro put her wine glass down on a side table and Jon took her into his arms. He used the slow dance as an excuse to pull her closer.

"Have I told you how lovely you look tonight, Caro?"

"Yes, but you can tell me again," she said and pushed a stray lock of his hair off his forehead.

He took her hand and turned his face into her palm and kissed it.

"Caro," he whispered tightening his hold on her as he turned her in the dance.

Her head was against his heart and she closed her eyes feeling the movement of their bodies, so perfectly aligned.

She tilted her head to look up at him.

Her eyes shone more green with darkening desire and they mirrored the desire in his as the song ended and a fast rock tune filled the air. All the younger cousins jostled for floor space and Jon took her hand and regrettably led her off the dance floor.

Jon watched the newly wed couple go through the pomp and splendor of the first dance, cutting the cake and looking into each others eyes as if no one else were in the room. It made him think of Caro. It made him think of marriage. They certainly weren't the bride and groom tonight but it had felt like they could be.

Maybe that's what weddings did to you, made you pliant for the fall. He hoped so. He hoped it made Caro feel as willing as he did to fall all the way into love…all the way into total commitment.

The joyous occasion and familial good cheer was contagious and filled the night with good feelings that flowed all around them and Jon could only hope Caro was feeling it too.

Caro found herself dancing, singing and laughing with all of Jon's relatives. By the evening's end, she was positively glowing with happiness. She didn't come from a big family. Like Jon she too was an only child and she'd never been part of so much good-natured fun and jovial frivolity.

When they cut the cake and Annette slapped a large creamy piece into Ben's mouth and smeared some of it onto his cheek she laughed as hard as anyone. And when they danced their first dance together she could see the love shinning in their eyes, and their eyes never strayed from each others. It was enviously wonderful.

The last song was announced and Jon took Caro's hand and walked her out to the dance floor. She leaned her head on his shoulder as they danced dreaming of someday having a wedding just like this one, and she didn't have one anxiety attack about imagining it.

The thought of a wedding with Jon was easy and sweet.

The final dance over, the candlelight flickering low on the flower adorned tables heralded the celebration was ending.

Caro didn't want to break the spell she was under; didn't want the evening to end. It was so unlike her to be this relaxed and comfortable with thoughts of forever running in head and yet she'd never felt more alive, more free…more like herself. Now that was an odd turn of words but it fit…and if it did then she truly loved Jon and she couldn't wait to tell him how she felt…or better yet show him.

Jon's parents, Paul and Jane Forbes cornered them just before they left the reception hall. His father had an appointment in the morning so they were driving home tonight and not staying over at the hotel where rooms had been reserved for the wedding guests.

"Caro it was lovely to see you again. You must come with Jon for a visit. Jon you be sure to bring her home with you next time," Jon's Mother insisted as she hugged Caro and then Jon.

"I'll do my best to bring her home...I promise," he smiled at his Mom but his words were for Caro.

"Of course I'll visit," Caro told Jon's mother but her eyes were on Jon. He was standing near his father and he looked so good, so tall, so strong and incredibly handsome.

Jon wanted to carry her into his hotel room and love her into the night and continue loving her even as the harsh light of day broke. The signals she was giving him were leading directly into that fantasy but he knew her desire was only surface tonight and he needed it to be soul deep and forever lasting.

Ironically, he was the one with all the doubts tonight.

They stopped by her room and he took her face in his hands and moved closer pressing her against the closed door.

"Do you know how much I want to follow you in there and love you to madness?"

"No, tell me," she smiled seductively up at him and her heart raced at the image he'd created.

"So much that I'm going to have to stand under a cold shower for a very long time before I can even think clearly...if then," he whispered against her lips before kissing her deeply, passionately and longingly. Her lips parted sweetly and he died a little inside as he tortured himself with more of her sweet taste before ending the kiss.

"Goodnight love," he murmured against her lips before he stepped back, his pulse dangerously unsteady as he walked away from her to the room next door.

Caro's eyes were closed but with the end of the kiss they flew open.

Jon had said Goodnight? Her brain wasn't connecting the words and the actions. She watched as he put the key card into his door. He was leaving her alone tonight?

"Jon? I didn't say no," she whispered not wanting the whole floor of the hotel to hear her.

"I know Caro…believe me I know…but parts of you have yet to say a resounding yes," he looked longingly at her before sighing deeply and walking into his room.

Commitment…he didn't have to say it but that was what he meant. Her fear of it hung between them. She should have told him she wasn't as afraid of a commitment with him but she hadn't told him, and now it felt too late.

She stared at his closed door and thought about walking over and knocking on it but the elevator down the hall opened on her floor and she saw several couples get off and begin walking down the hall so she quickly took her key card and opened her door.

CHAPTER 10

"So how was the wedding?" Nancy asked as she poured a strong cup of caffeine into Caro's nearly empty cup. "Did you and Jonathan remedy any of the frustrations?" She poured a second cup for herself and sat across from Caro.

It was Monday morning and a half hour before the café would open.

Caro had purposely come in early this morning because she had been so keyed up from the weekend. She needed to talk to someone and knew Nancy would be there early to set up the kitchen.

"It was a lovely wedding and Jon was dashing and handsome...but after...well, we had a good time the rest of the weekend. We spent time strolling in antique malls and eating at great restaurants. We had two romantic evenings together –"

"How romantic was it?" Nancy asked and leaned on her arms hoping for the good stuff.

"Not that romantic," Caro said with a resigned sigh and took a deep sip of coffee.

"Why not, it sounds like you were ready to go the distance."

"I was...but my distance still has a roadblock. Jon's goes all the way to eternity."

"Ahhh...so he wants marriage. Interesting guy, it's usually the woman who holds back sex for marriage."

Caro's mouth dropped open at her friend's insight and then she threw her napkin at her. "He isn't holding out. He..."

"Yes?"

Nancy waited for her to finish but Caro couldn't. Maybe Jon *was* holding out to make her realize it was all or nothing with him, and until she could get her head straight she was going to get nothing. "I don't know," Caro finished quietly, "I'm such a mess when it comes to commitments."

"You've been burned badly?"

"Not really. I honestly don't know what it is or why. I just run scared at the thought of forever with anyone. I don't think I have a lot of faith in it working out for a lifetime."

"Do your parents have a rough relationship?"

"No, they love each other very much. They're the perfect example of loving husband and wife and a long marriage. And as parents' they both love me."

"Well...I'm stumped, that's all the text book psychology I know, must be something subconscious then. Something must have happened and you've blocked it but it's built into your reactions even though you don't remember it."

"I can't even say it was due to Mitch and me because I was already afraid when he asked to marry me."

"Mitch?" Nancy interest was immediate.

Nancy hadn't gone to college with Caro and so she didn't know of that relationship. Caro thought back to that awful time and realized it didn't hurt so much to think about it anymore.

"Mitch was the one man I did allow to get close. He was everything I thought I wanted in a partner, attentive, loving, great sense of humor, real easy to look at."

"Sounds like Jon, all over."

Caro almost denied it but then paused and admitted, "Yes, I guess it does."

Mitch had been a lot like Jon but not as easy going and not as intensely caring as Jon. Those traits had not been in Mitch...but they were always in Jon. She'd never noticed it before but Jon was the blueprint she measured others by.

A revelation of sorts took hold. Jon was perfect for her, had always been perfect for her and if she could get over this fear of commitment, he'd be the one she'd marry.

Where had her fear of marriage come from anyway? She'd often wondered about it but never had a clue. Then suddenly she thought of Noah.

Uncalled for, the image of the man formed in her minds eye and she froze.

What the heck was it about that man? This was the second time it had happened...and why when she thought of marriage did she think of him?

Something pulled at her conscience. Something deep within her wanted to surface but she couldn't grasp it but Noah was somehow connected to her feelings, but why?

"So Jon is your perfect mate?" Nancy asked wisely.

"What?" Caro shook her head to clear it and focused back on her friend.

"I said…Jon is your perfect mate then."

"I don't know. I really don't know what's wrong with me," Caro's frustration was palpable.

"Don't work yourself up over it. Give it time. It's still new. Just give it time."

Caro nodded but she was still shaken by Noah's image and what it was that kept making her think of him and marriage.

*   *   *

It was the night the amateur astrology group met on the roof of the planetarium for stargazing and she was going to meet Michael and his mom for tonight's class.

Caro stepped out onto the rooftop of the museum and saw the group was already there and some were setting up their equipment.

Michael spotted her and called out.

Caro saw his mom standing beside him. This was the first time they were meeting although they had spoken on the phone about the outing.

Michael introduced his mom, Sara, to Caro.

"Thank you for inviting Michael and me to this event." Sara smiled gratefully.

"I'm so glad you were both able to attend," Caro said as she began to set up her telescope.

Michael already had his set up, the one that Caro had given to him the last time he'd visited the museum with his older brother Ted.

"Did Ted decide to stay home?" Caro asked Sara, "I was sure he would be here, he seems to have found a fascination with the museum."

"Yes, he has found an interest here but it isn't the museum. There's a young girl that works here and she's caught his attention."

Caro stopped positioning her telescope and looked over at Michael's Mom.

"Really, I wonder who it can be."

"I think her name is Madeline. I've heard him talking to his friends about someone named Madeline."

"She could be one of the high school interns that work at the museum's gift shop."

"I think you may be right," Sara nodded

Caro finished with the adjustments on the telescope she'd brought for Sara and looked through Michael's telescope. She made a few more adjusted to it and then stepped back.

"Your telescopes are all set up. Professor Ortega, will be giving a presentation to the group tonight and he gave me the coordinates for the viewing area M31, the Andromeda Galaxy, he'll be speaking about tonight. Now you can view the wonders of the night sky together."

"Thank you so much but how will I get the telescope back to you?"

"Just leave it with Professor Ortega. He'll put it away in the office for me."

"Thank you," Sara whispered sincerely.

"No thanks necessary. Just have fun."

Caro walked by several groups of other young would-be astronomers but paused when she spied Noah giving instructions to a small group of teenagers at the far end of the roof's terrace.

She stopped fascinated at the timber of his voice as he gave detailed instructions on positioning the telescopes. She listened to the enthusiastic way he spoke to the group and thought he had a way of mesmerizing his audience just as he had once said of her. His voice held reverence when he spoke of the vast universe and she was nothing less than impressed as she listened.

Requesting a white wine from a passing waitress she took a table and decided to stay.

Noah approached her as soon as his class concluded. He'd been aware of her all evening and could feel that she'd been focused on him as well.

"I couldn't help but notice you were listening attentively to my guidelines on discovering the universe. Was it that enthralling?"

"More like mesmerizing," she murmured ruefully. Still reeling from the shock of how much he held her attention and how connected she felt to him, uncomfortably connected.

"I take it you're not pleased with that?" he smiled knowingly and indicated the seat next to her, "May I."

"Sure…have a seat. I suppose we should talk about it."

Noah chuckled as he leaned on the table and looked into her less than romantic gaze. "Well I can assure you, it's been a kick in the head liking you too."

Caro's eye's widened at his candidness and then she laughed ruefully, "Yeah, I guess it has been at that, sorry."

"No apology needed. We've both been side swiped by this sudden attraction," his eyes no longer held any hint of humor; they were clear and penetratingly serious.

"I still can't act on whatever it is. I do have a boyfriend that I care deeply for."

Noah nodded and looked around the café. It was late and the other groups were ending their discussions. "Can we go somewhere to continue this talk? Maybe we can find a solution."

She shouldn't go anywhere with him. Jon might be calling her right now and he would worry about her and maybe there was a reason to worry.

No, she shouldn't go with him anywhere but she had to find out what was going on between them.

"Okay…there's a diner not far from here that has great cheese cake and good coffee, always a fresh pot."

"Sounds good, lead the way," he stood up and held his hand out to her. She looked at the strong tanned fingers extended to her and slowly placed her hand in his.

The feeling of familiarity was instantaneous and shook her to her very soul.

She knew exactly how his fingers would curve between her own, not the conventional handholding but a sensual blending of fingers. And when his thumb rubbed along the tender part of her wrist as they walked she wasn't surprised.

"Do you feel as if we've walked together before?" she asked quietly.

"I feel like I know your very soul Caroline and I can't say why," he stopped and looked down at her and when she looked up at him he wanted to pull her close, but he knew it would scare her. He knew the kiss would be everything he'd dreamed of but she wouldn't be able to handle it.

"I know you care for your boyfriend but couldn't we have a go at friendship. You do have room for another friend don't you?"

"Friends, you'd start a friendship with me?"

"I'd start anywhere you feel comfortable," his eyes dropped to her lips.

She felt the caress from his gaze and backed up because she felt compelled to lean into him, "I can handle friends," she quickly agreed and took her hand from his and walked briskly on to the diner, ignoring the awareness that was ricocheting between them.

Noah smiled, "Good. Then that's where we start...and where we end up," he shrugged and purposely left the rest of his thoughts unsaid.

The diner was crowded but they found a small table in a corner and ordered coffee.

They talked for several hours about their interest in astronomy and kept off the subject of the interest they held for each other. She didn't let him take her home but he waited while she hailed a cab and she couldn't stop the goodnight kiss he gave her as she tried to slip into the cab. It wasn't passionate but it had felt familiar and that was somehow worse.

*   *   *

The first floor of the Planetarium had been turned into a jazz café as it was every Friday night. Caro joined Nancy at one of the small tables set up beneath the large planet earth and soaked in the atmosphere of the planets above her and the night life all around her.

"So tell me have you talked to Jon about Noah?"

Caro had been looking up at the suspended planets and the lights that made them come to life at night but Nancy's question ended her frivolous thoughts and she lowered her gaze. "I don't know what to say. How can I tell him in one breath I love him and in the next there's another man catching my attention?"

"Are you going to spend time with Noah to see what the attraction is?" Nancy leaned closer and whispered the question.

"I don't think I have a choice anymore. I can't seem to stop thinking about him. Not like Jon...with Jon I feel this giddy newness but with Noah...When I'm around him I just know him...I don't know if that makes any sense but that's it ...I just feel like I know him."

"Are we talking intimately here?' Nancy asked with interest.

Caro began to shake her head but an image of him...of them flashed in her thoughts. She had never been intimate with him but, yes, it felt like they had a past. How strange was that?

"No...not intimate but weirdly enough it feels like I wouldn't be surprised by his lovemaking, like I would know that too."

"Whoa...that is too strange," Nancy shook her head and sipped her wine. "What does Noah say?"

"About the same thing, he can't explain what's between us but he isn't involved with anyone else so for him it's easy to decide to pursue this attraction, for me doing that could be the single biggest mistake of my life."

"Or not doing it could be," Nancy whispered to her.

Caro stared at her for a moment but then slowly nodded her head. She loved Jon. She really did, but what was between her and Noah could be something that needed to be developed before she could really say who she could love forever. If she ignored this she might always wonder about it and that could ruin the rest of her life and Jon's.

She still hadn't talked to Jon about Noah. How could she make him understand without hurting him?

The musicians began playing a jazzed up version of jingle bells and Caro realized it was nearing the Christmas Season. Thanksgiving was next week and what should have been a joyful occasion for her and Jon, discovering and developing their love, was now becoming a difficult time to live through.

"Don't worry Caro, what ever was meant to be will be. That's what my mom always told me you know, *que sera sera*, and for the most part I've lived by that. If Jon and you love each other this won't change anything, but you need to find out what attracts you to Noah before you can give your heart and soul to Jon anyway. So you need to talk to him. I think he'll understand. I don't think he'll like it, but you say he's been your best friend since forever…so he'll understand."

Caro nodded. Nancy was right she would have to talk to Jon.

"I can't believe it's only a little over four weeks to Christmas. The years get shorter and shorter when you're the adult who has to buy the presents," Nancy laughed trying to bring the night back into focus for Caro and give her a reprieve from the dilemma going on in her head.

"I know," Caro said but the tone of her voice was not happier, in fact it was sadder.

It just wasn't possible to make her feel better. The weight of what she had to do was not going to be lifted.

CHAPTER 11

(Council on High)

Orion watched the maze of events unfold for Caroline, Noah and Jonathan and wondered at the outcome for these three souls. He could see clearly the way they needed to go, but would they?

In his infinite wisdom, it was easy to determine the results of their emotions but they were in the mortal realm and very susceptible to all of its pitfalls.

Caroline needed to let go of the past and open up to a new beginning on a cleared life slate.

Dylan was a different concern, as Noah Bradley he'd lost his ability to see the path to self-knowledge before him. He needed to confront the subconscious desires of fulfilling his past life commitment to Angelica and his alternate desire for spiritual attainment.

Jonathon was the truest and most highly evolved being in the trio. His soul had been offered the highest attainment after each of his life's endings but each time he had decided to return to a new life, for in all his many lifetimes, he had always loved Caroline. The difference in this lifetime, he was finally ready to let her know.

What would come from the separate needs and desires of these three souls?

Orion could only guess. Freewill always had a hand in play and therefore all bets were off. But if they would look for their answers in the deepest part of their hearts and accept what they saw…then the outcome would most assuredly be 'perfect'.

*   *   *

Caro sat by her bedroom watching the snowflakes blowing gently across the rooftops of the buildings across the street. As the sun began to rise in the sky, she watched a new day breaking before her and with it her heart.

Yesterday, Jon had shared Thanksgiving Day with her at her parent's house but later that night she'd told him about Noah and the strange awareness that was happening between them, and Jon being Jon, her best friend above all else, said he understood. But unlike her Jonathon of yesterday, he didn't stay to talk about it. Instead, he kissed her goodnight and left her alone to realize she might have killed the best thing she'd ever had.

Caro sat there in the dawning hours without her best friend, the one person who could help her through the weirdness with his humor and logic. She was without him because she'd hurt him deeply and for what?

Yes, Noah was a handsome, possibly caring person but Jon was all that and more, much more, and yet when she thought of commitment, she saw images of

Noah. Why was Noah so prominent in her thoughts when she thought of marriage? *Was* he her true heart's desire? Or was life just throwing her a curve ball?

*   *   *

It was Friday night, the night Caro had agreed to see Noah.

He was due to arrive in five minutes and she wanted to meet him downstairs to avoid a possible run in with Jon. To that end, she rushed out of her apartment, pulling on her jacket and at the same time trying to align her apartment door just right so the key would turn and the lock would click closed. The alignment had been slightly off and she'd complained to Jack, the buildings maintenance guy, but he hadn't been able to fix it.

She was jiggling the key and losing the battle with her jacket, it was quickly slipping off her shoulders along with her purse and she was about to let them both fall when miraculously her jacket righted itself.

She clicked the lock closed and turned around.

"Oh Jon, Thank you," she smiled tentatively up at him. He was standing so close she breathed in his after-shave and it stirred her senses. He was freshly showered and looked utterly sexy. Her stomach quivered, they hadn't spoken to each other since a week ago last Thursday night.

"Going out?" he asked quietly.

She nodded. There was no need to elaborate; He knew tonight was her first date with Noah.

"Caro…" his voice faltered. He ran his hand through his hair and looked away from her shaking his head. "Never mind…I'll see you when you get back," he turned away to walk to his apartment.

"Jon?" she whispered, stopping him.

His eyes were dark with emotions when he turned back to her, his jaw was clenched and his handsome face was hardened with his effort to remain indifferent.

Caro could feel the tension between them and her heart ached. She reached out to touch him but he stopped her hand with his.

"Don't Caro!" his voice was harsh, "I'm not in a friendly mood unless you're planning to send Noah home?" his eyebrow lifted hopefully and he waited a heartbeat for her to say she would, but she remained silent.

"Guess not," he whispered as he stared into her eyes and then lifted her face to his.

The kiss was not sweet. It was pure passion wrapped in every intense need he was feeling and he bestowed it with full-blown desire. His tongue did not caress or request entry it demanded and took control, parried and tangled with hers until she moaned. His hands slid down her back but did not hold gently, they imprisoned with strength and needs.

Caro's head was spinning and her breathing was shallow. She opened her eyes to find Jon's intently upon hers making the kiss they were sharing all the more intimate.

A shaft of pure desire cut through her.

Jon ended the kiss slowly making her lean into him for more but his arms released her and he stepped back just as the sound of her apartment bell began to buzz.

"Now you'll have something to compare his kiss to," he said then turned and walked away. His stride was long and angry and within moments his door was locked between them.

Caro's eyes filled with tears as she leaned her head against her door.

She looked at Jon's apartment door and felt the chill of distance settle between them. He may have kissed her passionately but it had been laced with anger, something she'd never felt from Jon before.

She heard the buzzer ring again in her apartment and knew Noah was downstairs.

She glanced once more at Jon's closed door then walked slowly down the stairs wondering if she was making the biggest mistake of her life, and fearing she was.

They drove for quite a while on the Long Island Expressway. Caro wasn't paying much attention to where they were going, as she watched the landscape and thought of Jon. Noah noticed her quietness but didn't comment, letting her work out whatever was on her mind.

When he took an exit that led to Jones Beach she began to notice where they were.

"Where are we going?"

"There's a restaurant not far off the beach. They have great seafood and a view worth the ride," he reached over and squeezed her hand.

"That sounds …nice," she smiled back weakly.

"What's wrong Caroline?"

"Nothing and everything," she shrugged then turned away to look at the ocean as they drove over a drawbridge.

"Are you sorry that you agreed to see me?"

Caro looked back at him. His golden hair and the sun going down along the horizon cast what appeared to be a halo around his head. She smiled at the image. He had stolen into her thoughts, wrecked her composure and her relationship with Jon, so how could she picture him so innocently? But she did.

"No, I'm not sorry. I just wish I could figure out what it is between us or what it isn't. I don't know what's wrong with me."

"Nothing as far as I can see," he smiled and tried to break the serious mood, " and as for deciding between us ...I have to point out...you haven't given 'us' time together yet, so how could you even begin to compare?"

"Compare?" The word created an instant image of Jon's kiss and his parting words. "Yeah...how can I compare?" she replied casually to Noah and turned away to watch a lone sailboat gliding in the distant waters of the Atlantic and wished she was on it sailing far away from both men in her life, because she truly had no idea what she was doing anymore.

*   *   *

The week passed into two and she still had no understanding of her own feelings. It was awkward. How could her heart proclaim she loved Jon but was still attracted to Noah? She felt like the taffy in a taffy pull and it hurt terribly.

She'd spent the last Saturday afternoon with Noah. They'd had lunch and then walked in the park holding hands and talking like comfortable old lovers and yet they hadn't known each other very long.

She saw Jon Saturday night and he wasn't relaxed at all. She knew he wanted to question her about her date with Noah, but he didn't. She wanted to tell him everything she was feeling but she couldn't, and so they talked small talk, like casual acquaintances instead of the oldest and closest of friends, and the evening was extremely uncomfortable and she had never before been uncomfortable with Jon.

It was all so backward and the realization of what she was gambling with and what she could lose scared her.

When she mentioned her dilemma to Nancy she didn't think it was a dilemma at all. According to her, to have not one but two gorgeous men hounding after her was every woman's dream. She though Caro wasn't seeing the big picture and should be enjoying herself immensely and then in time she'd be able to decide.

Today was Sunday and she wasn't seeing Noah until the evening so she was going to spend this afternoon alone, and try to clear her head.

Her doorbell rang as she was buttoning up her coat to go for a walk and she bit back a curse. She didn't want to see anyone. Tentatively, she opened the door.

Her mom was standing in the hallway but her mom *always* called before coming over. Why was she here unannounced?

"Mom, is something wrong?"

"No, I was out shopping and thought I'd stop by."

"You were shopping where?"

"In Soho dear, there are a few stores I like there. I occasionally shop for...for art supplies."

"Art supplies?" The surprise couldn't be hidden in Caro's voice.

Her Mom blushed and nodded. "Yes dear. Your Mom likes to paint...surprised?"

"Yes, considering you've never shown me one painting."

"Can I come in and we can talk about it or were you going out somewhere?"

"I was just going to take a walk...would you like to join me? Have you had any lunch yet? There's a pretty decent diner nearby. I'll treat."

"I'd love to dear."

Her mom stepped back as Caro walked out into the hall and locked the door.

"So how long have you been painting?" Caro asked after the waitress delivered their order.

"I can't remember now when I didn't. It's been a long time."

"Why keep it a secret? I never saw you open a sketch pad…not once."

"No real reason …Well, maybe that isn't exactly true. My parents were perfectionists. I never quite met their standards for a daughter. It was hard to live with all the criticism, so I learned to never seek out any. It was easier to paint as long as I knew no one would judge it."

"I'm sure Dad encouraged—"

"I've never shown him my finished paintings."

"What?"

"You're the first person I've told these feelings to."

Caro stared wide-eyed as she asked, "Why not Dad?"

"I have no reason. I know he would have encouraged me. I know that he's a special man and I love him very much but the little girl in me still has a hard time opening up. Can you understand?"

"I guess so. Does Dad?"

"Yes, he knows me," was all she said but the way she'd said it made Caro wish that she were with Jon, completely with him because he knew her, understood her…so why did Noah, have the power to attract her? Something called to her when he was near, something deep within her acknowledged him even if she didn't want to.

Caro felt like she was going nuts and she wanted to cry.

"What's wrong Caro? You're not your usual happy self lately and I've noticed, and that's another reason why I came over here today. I hoped maybe you could talk to me about it." Sylvia reached over and squeezed her daughter's hand.

"I want to …I just don't know how. I don't know what's wrong with me."

"Tell me what the problem is."

"The problem is me...I think. You may as well know Jon and I have been dating-"

"I know."

"You know?"

Sylvia nodded. "So go on..."

"Well...we've been dating for a little while and I know I love Jon and not just as friends. I truly love him, but then I met Noah and it has been weird...I'm attracted to him too and now I'm seeing them both."

"Oh dear!"

"Yeah, oh dear is right. Jon's not pleased but he's giving me the time to figure this out. He wants me to be sure about us because he wants nothing less than a total commitment."

"He's a smart man. I've always felt he was the right one for you Caroline."

"I did too...until Noah."

"Tell me about him."

"He's compellingly handsome, the greenest eyes, so wise and sure of everything, including me. I mean he knows me. In every look I see myself in his reflection. Here's the strange part...I know him too and yet I don't know him at all. Sounds crazy right?" she put her head in her hands and nearly cried with frustration.

"It almost sounds like..."

"Like what?" Caro looked up at her Mom.

"Like maybe you've had a past with him."

"Mom, I've never met him before two months ago. Believe me. I'd remember him."

"What if he's a past life? Maybe there was a romance between you in another life."

Caro's mouth dropped open. Her mom believed in reincarnation? What next?

"You're kidding, aren't you?"

"I don't know...Who can say what came before the life we know. I've read a lot lately on that subject and there are so many opinions but frankly, no one knows for sure. So why couldn't it be that you and Noah have a past?"

"That's impossible," Caro shook her head but her voice held more question than conviction.

Sylvia leaned closer to her daughter and asked, "But wouldn't it explain an attraction to a stranger that feels like he isn't one?"

"Huh?"

"You know what I mean."

"Maybe, but what does that mean for Jon and me?"

"I think it's up to you to see which one you really love and then take the risk. I realize that's hard for you. You never jump headlong into anything; you study it from every angle before you make a move. You've always been cautious Caroline, especially with your heart."

It was true. She'd never been completely comfortable with anyone, except with Jon. He'd been her one true companion and she did love him beyond all else but still she held her heart away from him. Why? Was Noah the reason she hadn't given her heart completely to Jon? Was he the man she was waiting for? The man she could release her heart to? But Jon was her one love…and she did love him.

"My heart doesn't know which way to jump," she admitted in a quiet voice. "I don't know my own feelings."

"Then take your time and see them both for now. Make no decisions either way until you're sure."

"No chance of that. I couldn't make a decision to save my life right now."

"Relax dear. Time will give you the answer. I'm sure of it."

"At least one of us is," Caro smiled ruefully then bit into the sinfully rich chocolate cake her Mother had ordered her while she was spilling her heart out.

It had helped to talk about it and it was healing to share those confidences with her mom but it wasn't a cure.

She was seeing Noah in less than three hours and she was no closer to a solution.

CHAPTER 12

"Have some more wine," Noah topped off her glass and his, "You're very quiet tonight Caroline."

"I saw my Mom this afternoon and it was enlightening."

"In what way?" he leaned closer and breathed in the sea scent of her perfume, it drove him crazy and stirred a desire that was increasingly harder to keep at bay. He was desperate to move beyond friends.

"I've known my mother all my life-"

"I'm sure you have."

Caro laughed, "You now what I mean…Of course I've *known* her …anyway what I meant was that she never told me she liked to paint."

"Why is that?" he asked but his mind was on how the candle light shone in her eyes, he was so lost in wanting her he really wasn't listening to her response.

"Because she was afraid of criticism, she loves painting so much that if someone told her she wasn't good at it she'd have to stop. Isn't that sad?" Caro turned and, although his face was mere inches from her own, she didn't think he'd heard her.

"So many things are sad, Caroline…It's sad that I can't hold you closer or kiss you senseless. I want to feel your heart beat in time with mine all through the night and wake up to your breathing in my ear in the morning and love you again. It's sad it's not a reality."

Caro heard his softly spoken words as scenes played in her head, real or imagined, of the two of them wrapped in love and…she shook her head abruptly ending the provocative images.

"I think I've had too much wine," she got up quickly before he could stop her, "will you excuse me a moment?"

"Of course," he said as she walked away and he picked up his glass and downed the contents.

Caro walked into the ladies room. She stood looking into the mirror over the sink shaking her head. She was having dinner with a tiger, she thought, and quite possibly someone she'd shared a past life with according to her mother. Ridiculous of course but why had he felt so familiar and what the heck were those images about?

She hadn't had more then two sips of wine so she wasn't imagining anything. Those thoughts were clear and came with vivid memory recalls of intimate moments she'd never had with him.

Noah gave the evening up for lost when Caro fled from the table. When she returned, they ate in a stilted silence. When he drove her home he wasn't sure when they arrived at her door if he should just shake her hand and say goodnight, a kiss might drive her completely away from him.

Noah was lucky to find a space in front of her apartment building. He parked the car and turned to her.

"Would you be kind enough to offer this friend a cup of coffee before he hits the road again? I really could use the caffeine to stay awake."

His little boy act was cute and Caro was sorry she'd been such a basket case at diner tonight.

"Sure. Come on up, I'll make a pot of coffee."

They walked up the stairs quietly but the sound of their footsteps still carried to apartment 4B.

Jonathon reprimanded himself even as he pressed his ear against the door.

Was it Caro returning home? Or was it another neighbor?

She was driving him crazy. He didn't know how much more he could take of this but, knowing Caro, if she didn't figure out exactly what she felt for this Noah she would never give her self wholly to him, and to that end he'd wait…painfully he'd wait but even for Caro, he wouldn't wait forever.

Caro unlocked her apartment door and switched on the light.

Noah followed her in and just inside stopped and looked around.

The room was a welcoming shade of golden yellow. The couch, the main focal point, was enormous and appeared extremely comfortable, a great place to cuddle and watch a good movie, or make love he decided and smiled at the image he'd conjured. The color of it was not quite olive but close, definitely a color that would be comfortable in a forest setting.

He wasn't surprised by her taste. The natural colors fit her and he knew that.

"I'll make that coffee for us," she walked into the kitchen.

There was a small pass thru window between the two rooms and she spoke to him from there. "Make yourself at home Noah, this won't take long.

Caro set the coffee pot to brewing as Noah snooped more carefully around her living room.

He looked at the photos on her wall, picked up bric-a-brac displayed on shelves and absorbed the scent of her lingering in the room.

He felt, without seeing it, that her bedroom would be done in a warm earth tone as well. She was nature personified. Her scent was that of the ocean, her spirit that of air, hard to contain, and her body was fire... if he could get her to acknowledge their mutual need.

Unfortunately, her patience and stubbornness were like water, dousing his needs at every turn. He laughed at his bad poetry. He'd never before been driven to it by any other woman, but Caroline was different.

They were meant to be together, he was sure of that, now if only he could survive long enough for her to realize it too.

He turned as she came back into the living room carrying two cups of coffee on a tray.

"Who is this, your brother?"

Noah held up a framed picture of Caro and Jonathan as ten year olds on a day trip at the beach. "No...that's Jon," she placed the tray down on the coffee table.

"Interesting...so he isn't just your boyfriend he's been your best friend as well?" He asked and placed the picture back on the shelf.

"How can you know if he's been a best friend? We could have just been friends," she walked over to him and looked at the picture.

"Being a guy, I'd say if I were just friends with a girl since childhood we'd have gone our separate ways somewhere after high school ended but if I stayed around her after that...there was more than just friendship in my motives."

Caro stared at him, "Maybe you're right, but I wouldn't know about the 'being a guy' theory."

"Right," he mumbled and decided to change the subject because discussing Jonathan or 'Jon' at any age was counterproductive to his own motives. "Coffee smells great!" He smiled and walked her back to the couch, then sat down next to her.

"Thank you. It's a pure Kona coffee. I get it from a store at the South Street Seaport, Jon sometimes--" Suddenly her lips were pressed to his and she was held tightly against his warm hard chest. She thought to pull back but the kiss...the kiss was drawing her in, making her want something she hadn't had in a long, long, very long time.

Noah shifted drawing her even closer to him and deepening the kiss. His desire and need ran second to the feeling of rightness, the feeling of ...familiarity. He had been hungry for her, for what seemed like forever.

He felt her pulling back, "Don't," he whispered against her lips, "please don't move away."

Noah's voice was full of longing and Caro hesitated, stirred by a memory either real or imagined...but if she let him continue he would love her thoroughly and she would be shaking with wanting him. The image had her heart pounding but she didn't want to move into a complicated situation...and Noah's kiss *was* stirring feelings in her that she couldn't compare to Jon's. Comparing it to Jon's only confused her more.

She pushed her hands against his chest and broke the kiss.

"I'm not ready for this friendship to go further," she turned her head but Noah didn't let her deny what was happening.

"Tell me you don't feel it...tell me you don't imagine what it will be like for us and know you're not guessing."

"I can't," she told him honestly.

"Then please don't tell me to stop," he moved closer but she held her hand up to keep him back.

"Noah, please listen...even if I feel some pull of attraction to you...it doesn't mean I want to accept it. I'm not ready to act on anything I'm feeling-"

"Yet or ever?" he whispered but before she could answer him they both jumped at the sound of the door opening.

"Caro, I smelled that Kona all the way down the hall-" Jon stopped in the open doorway and froze.

Cozily sitting on the couch were Caro and Noah. He'd never expected she wouldn't be alone. How stupid of him not to have realized she'd brought him in for coffee.

"Sorry I intruded," he mumbled stupidly and turned to leave. He was nearly across the hall when he heard her call to him.

"Jon, wait!"

Caro had to run to catch up to him in the hallway, "Stay, please. There's plenty of coffee. Please join us."

"No thanks Caro. I'm not interrupting your date."

Noah fell back into the couch. He must be crazy to put up with this. Why was he so caught up in her and she was dancing around all that she felt for him? He got up and walked to the door.

"No you should stay," Noah was standing at her door now, "I was just leaving...I have a long drive home."

He stopped by Caro and Jonathan and a second of eye dueling occurred as they each sized up the opponent for Caroline's heart.

"Goodnight Caroline. I'll see you Monday at work." Then he passed the taller man and walked down the stairs.

Noah's footsteps echoed on the stairs as the silence stretched between them.

Jon had just seen his competition and it was too damn handsome and too darn real for him to ignore.

"Jon? Please come in." Caro's soft voice pleaded.

He knew he couldn't. He didn't want to hear all about her and Noah's evening. He'd had a taste of what it could be like between them, and it was killing him to be offered less.

He couldn't trust his own voice not to betray his emotions so he shook his head.

"Why?" she whispered.

He didn't answer her. He walked to his apartment and closed the door behind him sincerely wishing he'd never left it tonight.

CHAPTER 13

It was two nights after the fiasco of a date with Noah and the awkward ending with Jon.

Caro had avoided Noah at work on Monday and Jonathon seemed to be avoiding her. Out of desperation she called Nancy to come over. She needed to talk with someone.

"So tell me everything."

Nancy said as she sat on Caro's couch sipping a glass of white wine.

"If I don't figure out what's wrong with me soon I may lose both of them," Caro sat across from her on the large ottoman she used as an extra chair.

"Okay, so Noah isn't making you forget about Jonathan only complicating your life…and Jonathan isn't enough to make you forget Noah because you keep envisioning a life you may have had with him. Is that it?"

Caro nodded, "In a nutshell."

"Then I say pick one and just go for it. If the attraction lasts then you'll know you were right, and if it doesn't, then you can go back to the other."

Caro stared at her then blinked. "You are kidding me, right?"

"Maybe but then again, maybe it's exactly what you need to do. Shake your life up a bit. How can you know which one you want if you keep sitting on the fence with both of them? You've got to get involved with one of them to know for sure."

"I can't do that."

"Alright, but suppose you *had* to choose, suppose this was your last day to live and you had to choose someone to spend that day with. Close your eyes...Close them," she waited until Caro complied, "Now which one did you think of first? Quick, tell me!"

The first image Caro had was of Jon's laughing face but in a split second it changed into the intense stare of Noah's.

"Too close to call," she shook her head and sipped her wine.

"Oh no, it wasn't. Who was first?"

"Jon," Caro whispered.

"Then I'd say go for it with Jon," Nancy concluded and drained the wine in her glass.

"I think you've had too much to drink."

"I think you haven't had enough," she poured more into both of their glasses.

"Nancy, I don't want to make a decision like that because I'm emboldened with liquor."

"Fine...then make it because he's the right one for you. You keep saying how much you love him. Well, if Noah and you are only dabbling in friendship and Jon and you have moved beyond that...then I think Jon wins first try at winning your heart," Nancy said as she got up and walked into Caro's kitchen. She kept talking as she looked for something to nibble on. Wine always made her hungry. "Got any cheese?" she called out from the kitchen.

"So I'm supposed to go to bed with Jon to forget about Noah?" Caro asked as she walked into the kitchen and opened the fridge. She took out some cheese and put it on a cutting board.

"Sure! Makes sense to me...got an apple? Apples and cheese go good together."

"I think so," Caro took two apples from a fruit bowl on her counter, "but what about Noah? What if he's supposed to be the man I love?"

"You'll know if the fireworks aren't there with Jon and then you may as well go for Noah...got any chocolate? Chocolate is unbelievable good with cheese and apples and wine."

"Chocolate goes with all of that?" Caro asked as she looked for the bag of chocolate pieces she had in her cabinet.

"Absolutely...have I ever been wrong about anything?"

"I'm hoping not."

"Then you'll listen to my advice?"

"It must be the wine but somehow it's beginning to make sense...what about grapes do grapes go with this snack?"

"Grapes with wine are you kidding? That would be overkill. Do you want to ruin the taste?" Nancy grabbed the tray laden with crackers, cheese, cut apples and squares of bittersweet chocolate and carried it into the living room.

Caro followed shaking her head at what she was contemplating. "I don't think I can do what you suggested even if it made sense," she confessed as she sat down on the ottoman.

"It's my best solution," Nancy chewed thoughtfully on a chunk of cheese, "You've got to get beyond the first stage to know if it's a lasting relationship."

"But one of them will be hurt."

"Life is painful Caro and they're both big boys, they can take it. You aren't doing either of them any favors by dangling the carrot in front of both of them. You have to decide."

"I know that and I don't want to be fickle but I don't intend to jump into bed with anyone until I'm ready to commit to a life with them. To be true to the love I have in my heart but...I think you're right about one thing. I do have to focus wholly on one at a time. It's the only fair thing to do...but which one?"

"My vote is for Jon," Nancy pulled her feet up under her on the couch and sipped thoughtfully on her wine.

"Why do you say Jon?" Caro was curious to know why Noah didn't floor her. He was simply gorgeous and successful in his field. Usually that was what Nancy said she wanted from a mate herself.

"Well...Noah I admit is perfectly gorgeous, powerful and smart but I think I prefer the vulnerability in Jon. He's successful too but he's also insightful and true and just a bit more down to earth. Those 'too perfect' kind of guys always make me feel like less...but that's just me kiddo...Truth is, you've got to decide this one for yourself."

"Yeah I guess I do..." Caro answered softly, her mind reeling with Nancy's summation of the two men in her life. 'Perfect' did fit Noah and 'down to earth' sure was Jon, and those descriptive words touched a chord in her too.

She tried to pull the thread of what she was feeling forward but couldn't. It was like she had the solution but it was under water and she was unable to reach it.

All she knew was that somewhere deep inside herself she felt and knew more about why she was so confused.

"Hey Caro?"

"What?" Caro turned expecting more advice.

"I don't think I'm going to make it home."

Nancy confessed as she drained her glass," I shouldn't have had so much wine.

"Don't worry," Caro laughed, "I'll fix us some sandwiches and that will soak it up," she stood up and teetered a second realizing she was a bit unsteady herself.

"Yeah it'll soak it up in about three or four hours."

"No problem...the couch is comfortable and you're welcome to stay. You'll fit in my stuff so just pick something from my closet in the morning."

Nancy shook her head. "I can't believe this...I feel like a high school kid hanging out, drinking wine, and talking about boys."

"I can top that, I feel like a high school girl with a crush on two guys and too green to know what to do about it," Caro picked up the tray.

"You win!" Nancy agreed and they both laughed.

Caro brought the tray and Nancy brought the empty bottle of wine into the kitchen.

Caro fixed two sandwiches, piling everything that was in her lunchmeat tray on them. It took both hands to hold them as they ate.

As the hours passed they talked about everything and by midnight they'd decided they felt less affected by the wine they'd had.

"I think I can sleep now." Nancy admitted and curled into the comfy cushions of the sofa mumbling, "I'll make the breakfast in the morning," and then she fell quickly into a deep sleep.

Caro put a blanket over her friend and shut off the lights before going into her room.

She had no new solution to her problem but she did feel better having talked it out with Nancy.

The next morning Caro woke up to the smell of bacon frying. It reminded her of Saturday mornings when she was a kid. On weekends, her mom always made big breakfasts for her and her Dad.

She snuggled deeper into her pillow breathing in the rich tantalizing aroma. Her stomach grumbled and the daydream ended.

She opened her eyes and stretched before pulling herself from her bed and going to take a shower.

The water woke her up completely and something from last night's conversation rang true for her. She did have to decide to see only one of them and she realized she had made a decision last night.

It would be Noah.

He was the one she knew less about and the one who provoked unknown depths of feelings in her. He was the mystery she had to solve before she could decide whom to give her heart to.

She finished showering and dressed.

Caro admitted she felt better having a plan and now she couldn't wait to dig into that wonderful smelling breakfast and tell Nancy what she'd decided.

As for Jon, she would have to tell him too but she might wait a few days to workout the best way to say it.

In the kitchen, Nancy was not alone.

Jon had smelled the bacon as well and thought Caro might burn the apartment house down so, even though things had not been resolved between them, he'd come over to investigate. Seeing that it was Nancy, a bona fide cook, he turned to go but she stopped him with a plate full of food and invited him to stay.

Of course, at the sight of the fluffy eggs, crisp bacon, and warm buttered toast he couldn't have turned away if his life depended on it.

"Good Morning!" Caro called out as she breezed into the kitchen then stopped short as she noticed Jon at the table. "Hi," she finished weakly.

"Good morning to you," he saluted a fork full of eggs in her direction purposely making his tone light and casual, "I'm sorry if I'm imposing on a girl talk morning but Nancy used brute force to get me to stay."

Caro's stomach relaxed at his friendly smile. Maybe he forgave her for the uncomfortable ending the other night. Maybe he would even understand her decision… No, he wouldn't, he wouldn't understand or want to see her in another man's arms…but at the moment he was being Jon, the Jon she knew and loved, and she would not stir the pot of trouble this morning.

She smiled genuinely at him then bent down to eat the eggs off of his fork.

"Mmmm that is great. If I didn't already have an invite to this breakfast feast, I'd have found a way in myself."

Jon pulled his plate closer for protection and glanced at Nancy, "I was thinking…is there any chance you'd consider moving into this apartment house and having friends over for breakfast every morning?"

"Not likely, so enjoy it while you can…grab a plate Caro dig in before Jon finishes it all," Nancy advised good-naturedly as she sat down at the table.

"I can't help it," Jon said defensively, "Caro can't boil an egg much less scramble one...although now that I think about it…her boiled ones kind of look scrambled."

Caro slapped his arm playfully.

"I'm not that bad," she declared but when neither of them defended her she had to agree maybe she wasn't very culinary but she had other traits. "Well, so what, so I'm not the best cook, big deal," she held up her hand when it looked like Jon might add to that,

127

"Alright, I'm not a cook period, but you must like something about me or you wouldn't hang around right?"

Jon's fork froze midway to his mouth and he turned his attention to her. In his peripheral vision he knew Nancy was watching so he couldn't really answer but the silly remark had brought all of his feelings to the front. They needed to talk and soon. He couldn't put up with this arrangement much longer. What he hoped was that Noah was no longer a consideration in her life but he couldn't say any of this with Nancy here. He could only stare at her and murmur, "Yeah, there're a few reasons," then he picked up his coffee cup and refilled it. "Anyone else?" he asked as he held up the coffee pot keeping the mood light around the table.

Nancy and Caro decided to call a cab to make it to work on time. When the cab was downstairs, Jon told them to go on and leave, he'd do the dishes for them, now that he had real sustenance to fuel his energy.

Nancy walked out of the apartment first and Jon took that moment to pull Caro back for a long kiss.

"I need to see you tonight. We have to settle this," he whispered when he left her lips to kiss the tender spot on her neck.

Reluctantly, Caro agreed to see him tonight, but when she told him her decision she knew there was a very good chance it would end their friendship forever.

She heard the horn blow, the cab was anxious to leave but she took Jon's face in her hands and pulled him back for a long and passionate kiss, he didn't hesitate to pull her closer too. She knew he might be thinking they were going to be alright when in fact, she was taking what she hoped *wasn't* her last kiss goodbye.

CHAPTER 14

"Are we alone?"

The question reverberated through the space theater and Caro leaned back to absorb the feel of the night sky above her. She'd decided to stay with her school group today and enjoy the show. She hadn't watched it since before she started working here. The last time had been nearly a year ago when she had dragged Jon with her. He'd enjoyed it so much that he even used the experience for one of his comic strips.

In the strip, Cal and Ivy were on a school outing to a planetarium and Cal carried in his pocket a happy face flashlight that could project the little smiley face onto anything. When the moon appeared in the night sky above him, little Cal flashed the face on it and yelled, "Look there he is! It's the man on the moon!"

Caro smiled remembering the cute cartoon, and looked around her wondering how many of these angelic little children might wish to do the same?

Seeing the rapt attention on their faces as they looked up made her look up too.

The Narrator's voice drew the audience beyond earth's solar system, far beyond, until our solar system was nothing more than a distant light in the universe.

The vastness of it took her breath away and as always it put her life back into perspective.

"We're just a blip in the universe, having our moment in time and projecting it far out into the reaches of space. Never knowing just where those reaches end. Never knowing if any other life form would be receiving those blips." She'd said that to Jon when they'd watched the show together last year. He'd smiled at her and joked, "Well if their listening right now they'll know that one of these blips is darn hungry 'cause my stomach is growling loud enough to break the sound barrier."

Jon also had a way of helping her keep her life in perspective. He had a way of neutralizing her worries and making her enjoy each day for what it was worth. So why did she have this attraction to Noah? If Jon made her life so full and happy why did Noah distract her from that life?

The sounds of the children squirming in their seats alerted her to the end of the show. Sure enough, the night sky above them was growing lighter. The space show was over and Caro had to lead the group of children through the rest of the museum tour.

All her questions still unanswered just as the questions of life in the universe.

Maybe later, maybe much later, she would find her answers but she could almost bet it would be easier to find life in the far reaches of space.

"Hi Caroline mind if I join you?"

Noah had his hand on the seat across from her at the café's table. She couldn't say no but she really wasn't ready to see him yet. She had wanted to have a relaxing lunch but it wasn't meant to be.

"Sure," she smiled up at him.

"I've been trying to catch up with you but you've been very elusive."

"Me?" she frowned.

"I won't ask why. I only wanted to invite you this weekend to a 'star party' on the beach near my home. I think you'll enjoy it if you come."

"Really, you're having a star party on the beach?"

"Yes, really," he laughed at her open suspicion, "I have a few colleagues that will be setting up their telescopes and allowing viewing during the evening."

"That actually sounds great. I'd love to view the night sky from the beach. When is it?"

"It starts Friday night as the sky gets to that perfect darkness and again on Saturday night. We'll be home by Sunday afternoon."

"Over two nights?" her voice lost its excitement.

"Yes, it's the whole weekend. They set up the equipment for a two-night viewing. We chart and take notes the first night and compare them through out the day and then review each others findings the next night…I guess that's probably too boring for you."

"Noah Bradley how could you say that? I love the mathematics of space as much as I love viewing the beautiful cosmos. Of course I would die for a chance to be among several professionals in the field of astrophysics but …Overnight? Is there a hotel nearby?"

"You can stay at my house Caro. There will be plenty of room and two of the professors and their wives will be staying too. If you're worried about my intentions I assure you, even though I would love to spend the night gazing at stars and the break of day gazing into your eyes, I realize you want us to start as friends and, as friends, I thought we could explore our mutual interest in astronomy as a way of furthering our friendship and attraction."

Caro bit her lip wanting to say yes but still reluctant to accept but her mind screamed that she wanted to go and she wanted to go very badly. She'd never been to a star gazing party and this was not a chance to pass up lightly.

"Yes, I'd love to go. When do we leave?" she decided and couldn't hide her enthusiasm.

"The traffic to Long Island on the weekend is usually bumper to bumper so if you wouldn't mind leaving early from work on Friday we could go that afternoon."

"I don't usually have groups on Fridays but sometimes I do. I'd better check my schedule."

"I already did. You're free of school groups this Friday."

"But I also have to get the time off approv-"

"It's already approved if you want it. Professor Grant felt it would be a good experience for you as well," he leaned on his hands and waited for her answer.

"It seems you've thought of everything," she murmured, not sure if she was comfortable with that or not but the excitement overshadowed her caution. "I guess it's all set then," she grinned at him.

"Great," he murmured, his voice husky.

Caro nervously glanced down at her watch and realized she was going to be late catching up with her group by a few minutes.

"I'd better run," she got up and began to walk away from him.

"Caro wait!"

She turned back to him.

"Be sure to pack a bathing suit."

She tilted her head as if she wasn't sure she'd heard correctly. "Pack a bathing suit? Isn't it a little cold in early December for swimming in the ocean?"

He laughed. "I imagine it would be unless you're a polar bear but I have a hot tub with a skylight above it. I thought you might enjoy relaxing in it and viewing the night sky from there as well."

Caro stared into his sea-green eyes and was held by the erotic power of them. She could almost feel the throbbing water around them and his strong body close beside her.

"I'll think about it," she answered noncommittally and turned away. The truth was, she would think about it, probably all day.

*   *   *

Jon stared at the blank board in front of him. He couldn't think of one usable story line for Little Cal and Ivy. His thoughts too wrapped around his frustration with Caro. The world outside his window was always a myriad of new ideas. The whole reason he'd positioned his drawing board in front of the window was to people watch. It was usually great for helping him create, but not today.

Today, he'd been sitting here doodling and romanticizing a future with Caro. He'd penciling a house complete with the proverbial white picket fence. He'd lovingly created three little children of varying ages chasing a puppy in the front yard and then highlighted in a shaft of sunlight he drew Caro laughing at their antics. When he drew himself into the family picture he stared at it for a long time then crumpled it up and tossed it in the trash can that was already overflowing with similar scenarios.

He kicked over the small wastebasket venting his frustration. He had to talk to her tonight he couldn't take the suspense anymore. If she wanted him, he needed to hear it. If she wanted Noah …He'd rather not know.

He broke his pencil in half and decided he needed a walk.

Caro had dawdled as long as she could. She'd window shopped for hours before taking the train home. Now she stood outside her building and hoped she had the courage to explain to Jon why she was going to spend the weekend with Noah.

"Afraid to go in?" the deep voice tickled the back of her neck. Her heart ached, as she turned to Jon.

"No just not ready to go in yet, the weather is so…"

"Freezing?" he supplied, "Blisteringly cold?"

"No…exhilarating," she lied and her teeth chattered.

"You have a strange attraction to the cold Caro. Come on I'll walk you inside. Maybe the cold has frozen your extremities and you can't tell you're at risk of losing them," he took her arm and led her into the building.

Silently they walked up the flights of stairs, when they reached their landing she turned to him.

"Did you have dinner yet?" she asked hoping he hadn't. Maybe they could go somewhere to eat. Around a crowd she might be able to talk to him, but not alone.

"Yeah…I had roast pork and asparagus and if you ask real nice I may be persuaded to share the left over with you."

She sighed and began to walk to her apartment. Jon pulled her back to him. They were standing in the hall outside his door.

He didn't say a word at first just stared at her then slowly, ever so slowly, he moved forward until she was against the door to his apartment.

"On second thought Caro...you don't even have to ask. I'd share that and more if you only hinted at wanting it...or me," he whispered the last words.

Caro was emotionally moved by his words. Something deep within her responded and, almost with a will of their own, her arms encircled him and her lips answered him.

Her heart pounded against his and she felt weightless and wanting. The door opened behind her but she didn't fall because she was swept up into his arms. He kicked the door closed and carried her into his bedroom. Gently he laid her upon the bed and sat beside her. She reached for him but he took her hands in his and shook his head.

"I want you because I love you. I've always loved you and I've waited for the day when you'd see me as someone you could love and someone you could spend your life with and not as just a friend. So I need to know Caro...do I have a chance for that dream to come true or has Noah awoken something in you more powerful than what we share?"

Caro was weak with desire and the man she desired was Jon but slowly his words penetrated the fog and she remembered she was going to spend the weekend with Noah. She was going to the Star Party with him and she had to tell Jon...she didn't want to tell Jon. She gazed into his golden brown eyes, not wanting to ever tell him and decided she would tell Noah it was off. She wasn't going with him, she was choosing Jon.

In the distance, a phone rang and Caro knew instinctively it was hers. She turned her head to listen.

Jon tensed, "Don't even think about it. You have an answering machine."

"Jon, I have to, it could be important!" she jumped off the bed and headed out of his bedroom.

Jon followed close behind her as she ran to her apartment trying to get her keys out of her purse but by the time she got her door open, the phone had stopped.

Caro stood in the open doorway just as her answer machine prompted the caller to leave a message.

"Hi Caroline…I just wanted to remind you we'll be leaving early Friday afternoon so bring your suitcase to work, we'll leave from there. Call me when you get in and we'll firm up our plans for the weekend. I wish you were there I'd…I'd like to hear your voice...so call me back…bye."

Jon was right behind her and the silence felt like death and maybe it was because when she turned around, his expression said it all.

"No! Jon please listen to me, it's not what you think. It's a star gazing out on Long Island and a lot of professional people will be there, not just Noah," she pleaded but he backed away.

"I'll see you after your weekend Caro," he said without emotion and walked back to his apartment. Caro heard the lock slid into place and her heart shattered. She walked into her apartment and sat down on the floor of her living room and cried for hours. She cried until there were no tears left to cry, but even then she found no answer.

Sometime in the night she dragged herself to bed and slept without dreaming.

In the morning, her head pounded and she brewed a strong pot of coffee. After three cups she decided she had to see Jon she couldn't leave it this way between them. She needed to tell him she wasn't going to the star party.

Caro walked across the hall to Jon's apartment and knocked but there was no answer, she called his name, still no answer. Was he avoiding her? She went back to her apartment and got the key he'd given her.

When she entered his apartment she found he really wasn't there. His bed was perfectly made and the apartment felt as if he hadn't been there all night and somehow she knew that was true but where had he spent the night?

She called his cell phone and it went straight to voicemail. It never went to voicemail. Jon always answered. Where was he?

Caro called in sick for the first time since she'd started working at the museum.

Professor Grant told her to feel better.

Noah left a message in the late afternoon but she didn't return it.

Jon had not returned home.

It was nearly five in the evening when she thought she heard footsteps in the hall hoping it was Jon she flung her door open wide and looked out into the hall. It was Mr. Greene who lived on the floor above them. He was passing her door on his way to the next set of steps. "Hi, Caroline, you're home early today aren't you?"

"Hi, Mr. Greene, I decide to take a day for myself."

"That's okay; it's even good to do that once in a while…enjoy your day."

"Thanks," she mumbled, disappointed and more worried then before. She returned to her apartment and as she passed by her phone noticed her message light flashing. She pressed the button wondering when she'd missed a call.

At the sound of Jon's voice she turned up the volume.

"Hi Caro…It's me…sorry I left like that but I swear it was that or drag you back to my bed and love you until you couldn't remember that guys name…" A deep sigh came over the machine and Caro fell into the chair near the phone shaking as she listened.

"I don't know what plans you've made but I know you have to figure this out. When I left you I got in my car and drove for hours. I didn't know where I was going... I just needed to keep moving...After a while I realized I'd driven to New Jersey so I went to my parent's summer house near Seaside Heights...remember all the great summers we spent there when we were kids?" there was pause and then he said, "anyway...you know it's where I go when I have writer's block but don't worry about me...I need some time to work things out too...I'll see you Sunday night and we'll talk--"

The message clicked off and Caro stared at the stupid machine wondering if Jon had finished his thoughts or if the tape had just run out.

She wished he were home. She needed to see him, needed to talk to him. She hurt so much inside she didn't feel like she could survive it. She felt numb and didn't want to move but then her phone rang and she grabbed it.

"Hello?" she yelled into the phone.

"Hi, yourself, I hope that's excitement for my call I hear."

"Oh, Noah, it's you."

The excitement wasn't for him. The change in her voice made that apparent.

"I guess you were expecting someone else to call?"

"I was.... Jon went on a trip and I thought he might call."

"I see...do you want to cancel coming with me tomorrow?"

His disappointment carried through to her. She really thought about it and if Jon were here she would have but this weekend together could help her figure out what was between them. And she wanted to do that before Jon came home.

"No, I'll go."

"You'll have to hold back the excitement I don't think I can take it."

"I'm sorry...I just haven't felt well today," she sounded so drained that Noah felt instantly contrite. "I'm sorry Caroline. Can I bring something over for you? I know a delicatessen that makes a great chicken soup. I could be there with a hot container in half an hour...just say the word."

"No thanks. It's sweet of you to offer but ...I'll be all right. And don't worry I'll be ready tomorrow."

CHAPTER 15

Jon walked along the surf in the early morning light. The cold sharp sting of the ocean in December should have chilled his desire for Caro but it only made him dream of holding her closer to stimulate warmth.

"What was she doing? More precisely what were they doing?"

He'd had less than an hour of sleep last night. He'd dreamed of her in so many different scenarios. As his wife, as his friend, as someone else's wife, and then he woke up and tossed for the remainder of the night.

As the sun rose higher in the sky he walked along the shoreline searching for some answer to his torment.

A man standing near the breaking waves caught his attention.

The man was casting a line into the churning freezing ocean. He'd never catch anything in those cold rough waters this close to shore, Jon thought, but he walked closer to watch.

"Howdy!" the man drawled reeling in his line and then casting it again. He had a hat shading his eyes as he turned but his smile was friendly.

"Hi!" Jon smiled in return, "What are you trying to catch?" He couldn't help asking, his curiosity was peaked.

"Oh, I don't much care what it is…I like surprises."

Jon nodded thinking the man must mean it, for it sure would be a surprise if anything tugged on his line except maybe an odd seashell.

"Have you been fishing here long?"

"Nah…just about an hour is all."

The man pushed up the brim of his hat and turned to him, his eyes a serious gray caught Jon off guard. They were the wisest eyes he'd ever seen, swirling depths of knowledge. Where had that thought come from? Jon blinked and laughed at himself for his ridiculously whimsical thought. "Have you ever caught anything here? I mean in this cold churning surf and this close to shore?"

"Sure have," the man pointed to a small cooler next to him, "See that…most days I fill it to the top with fish, all kinds of fish."

"Really…that's remarkable." Jon thought it impossible but he didn't say that.

"You don't believe me do you?" The man smiled knowingly.

Jon was again drawn to the power of his gaze. "I wouldn't say I don't believe you…but maybe I'm a little skeptical."

"Understand," the man nodded. "You just watch and learn then. You know you don't always catch a fish in the prime locations and just as it is true you should know that you can catch them in the unlikeliest places as well...and with very unpredictable weather conditions and the strangest bait."

The man reeled in his line and the hook held a tiny piece of what looked to be some kind of meat.

The man reached into his pocket and took out a larger piece and whispered, "My secret is hotdogs," he said and then cast his line in again.

"You're fishing with hotdogs for bait at the freezing shoreline?"

"Yup!" he said confidently.

"How about I buy us some lunch and this way you won't go hungry this afternoon, just incase the strange conditions are too much for the fish," Jon said with honest concern.

"How about I cook you some fish for lunch?"

"Sure I'll go to the market and buy some and we can cook it."

"Oh ye of little faith," the man mumbled under his breath and then had to pull back on his fishing pole as it started to bend. "You've snagged your line on something." Jon eyed the tugging line oddly.

"Yeah, I'd say it's at least a four pounder."

"No way!" Jon's eyes widened as the man reeled in a healthy looking specimen then watched as he took him off the hook and threw him back in the surf.

"You got a name doubting Thomas?"

Jon laughed and held out his hand, "Yeah it's currently mud but before that it was Jonathan...most friends call me Jon."

"Howdy, Jon," he took his hand in a warm, firm and comforting grip, "My name is Oscar and most people call me...Oscar." he laughed and pointed to a second folding chair next to his. "Join me Jon you might learn a thing or two about fishing."

Jon sat down on the chair he indicated and as he watched him fish they talked.

Jon learned that Oscar had lost his wife the year before. He'd come to his beach house for solitude and fishing and after a time the beauty of the sunrise and the power of the ocean crashing on the shore helped him to see that his life still had meaning. He knew his wife was in spirit somewhere beyond his reach but someday he would be with her again. Once he realized this he noticed that as each day passed his desire to live grew and so did his ability to fish nearly anywhere he threw his line. He felt it was life's way of giving him back something for having taken away his laughter, his love, his Carolina.

Jon stared at the man. "Your wife's name was Carolina?"

"Yes but I called her Caro. She was pure sunshine," his eyes misted over and he smiled weakly, "How I miss her."

"I am so sorr-."

"No please. No sorrow necessary. I had forty five wonderful years with my Caro and I know someday we will be together again. It's my faith and I am happy today and she is in my heart, always...but I look at you and I see deep sorrow. Have you lost someone?"

"No...maybe. Yes, I suppose I have." Jon felt his heart open and his story and Caro's flowed out. The man listened intently and when he finished Jon felt lighter, a hundred pounds lighter, for having shared his burden with this stranger.

Oscar sat there in the waning sunlight intently listening to Jon's story until they both realized it was nearly three.

"I'm sorry I went on like that. I can't imagine what got into me," Jon felt embarrassed but Oscar shook his head.

"Never apologize for needing someone to talk to son. I'm proud you chose me. I wish I had some way of making that little girl see what she has right before her eyes but I think, if I'm not mistaken, she will."

"I'm not so sure-"

"Trust me. Your qualities are your beacon, they shine out from inside you and the woman who loves you will be drawn to them like a ship in a fog finding the lighthouse. She'll crash on your shore soon enough I'll be betting ...real soon," he slapped Jon on the back then stood up to stretch. "I'd better be heading home the sun is weakening and my bones are chilling."

"Will I see you tomorrow?" Jon felt like a kid begging a parent to stay.

"I'm afraid not son, today was my last day here. I've sold my beach house. I no longer need it...but you take care now. Remember have faith in her finding her way to you."

"Sure, I'll keep a light on, right?" Jon smiled and folded up the beach chairs and walked with Oscar to the boardwalk. "I'll help you carry these to your beach house."

"No...I'm not such an old coot. I brought them here I can get them back. I only live up those steps. Thank you for asking though, you've got a good heart Jon and it will win you a good life."

Jon handed the chairs to Oscar and watched the older man walk up the steps to the boardwalk. He walked straight and tall never faltering with his load and he had to be in his seventies but appeared as strong and agile as a young man. There was a lot he could learn from Oscar, maybe he'd already learned.

His life wouldn't end if Caro didn't choose him. He would learn to go on without her and those drawings he'd been avoiding back at his apartment needed to be created. His life simply had to get back on track. He'd made a decision this afternoon too. He would be going home. He was ready to face his life...and more than that, he was ready to accept his life what ever it held for him and whatever or whoever it didn't.

*   *   *

The drive out to Noah's beach house on Montauk took nearly three and a half hours with the traffic on the Long Island Expressway. They'd just turned onto the Montauk Highway and Caro was antsy to be out of the car.

Her thoughts during these long hours had been solely focused on Jon. She was having a hard time ignoring the feeling of deep loss his leaving had caused her. She hadn't been a good conversationalist for Noah on the long drive either but he thought she was still feeling under the weather, and she let him believe that.

"We're finally here," Noah proclaimed as he pulled into a long circular driveway.

Caro had her first view of Noah's house.

The large two-story house was starkly beautiful as it rose up from the beach and pointed its wide slanted roof to the heavens. Several skylights were visible to her at this distance and she knew instinctively that they had been placed in prime viewing locations for each season of the night sky.

"Fascinating," she whispered.

"I like it," he said simply.

"Did you have this built?"

"My brother Joshua is an architect he helped me design it and the firm he works for built it for me."

Caro turned to him, "You have a brother?"

"Actually I have two younger brothers and one older sister...correction she's only slightly older... just two years, she's thirty one and she hates being the oldest."

145

He glanced over at Caro and smiled at her wide-eyed gaze, "You look surprised."

"I...I didn't know you came from so large a family. I guess I know very little about you."

"That's not true, you know a great deal about me. It's my family you know very little about," he said with simple assurance.

He was right. Something inside of her knew him and that was what this weekend was all about wasn't it?

"I suppose so," she agreed and then opened the car door not wanting to continue that line of reasoning. She did need to explore what was between them but Jon had been on her mind the whole drive and her worry about him had not lessened.

Noah watched her retreat. Obviously, she would not fall gently into his arms, and his hope for this weekend that it would lead to a closer relationship wasn't looking good either. It could change though...it only depended on her accepting what she felt for him.

He gave a deep sigh of frustration and began to unload the suitcases from the trunk.

They began walking up the path towards the house just as the front door opened and a petite dark haired woman with sparkling blue eyes stepped out to greet them.

"Hello Noah," she smiled brightly, "this must be Caroline."

The woman extended her hand to Caro who took it tentatively.

"I'm Noah's sister Miranda and I can see by the surprise on your face that my brother hasn't told you I live here."

"No, he hadn't," Caro smiled back genuinely relieved that she wouldn't be completely alone with Noah this weekend.

Miranda raised her eyebrow, "Typical brother," she shrugged and guided Caro into the house, "Well, come on in both of you it's chilly out here and I have a nice fire burning in the fireplace warming the living room to toasty perfection."

Caroline followed her hostess but stopped short just inside the entrance. The interior was as breathtaking as the exterior had hinted at. She stood there marveling at the height of the room as Miranda continued on into the large sprawling living room. There was a curving staircase leading up to a second floor balcony that surrounded three sides of the room. The fourth side, she noted with a thrill all its own. It was a glass wall that framed the beautiful Atlantic Ocean just beyond the house, no picture from any master painter could have done this room more justice. The ten foot Christmas tree with its lovely lights and ornaments added a festive touch to the natural beauty framed outside the window.

"Absolutely beautiful," Caro spoke with true reverence in her tone, "It's like living outside but being completely and comfortably protected from the elements."

She felt the warmth seep into her from the flames flickering in the fireplace and knew she could easily see herself living in this house. It was that welcoming feeling that comforted her but there was something more to her feelings that was not so comforting. She felt as if she and Noah had once lived in a home with another natural setting around them and that feeling clearly hinted of a past life together. Had her mother been correct in her assumption had she and Noah lived a life before this one? It certainly wasn't an easy thought to have and she didn't want to dwell on it at all so she was very glad when Miranda broke into her thoughts.

"That's exactly why I like it. And why I told Noah I would always land here whenever I wasn't working. I'm a marine biologist and I love being at the ocean anyway so when I'm not traveling around the globe I roost here. It works out well...my brother can't take care of this place alone and our younger brother Josh is twenty-four and married and has a place of his own down the beach but very little time to check on this place. And then our youngest brother Zachary is only twenty, and well ...I guess you could say he's too young and carefree right now to be held responsible for much and Noah wouldn't trust him to spend the weekend here alone."

"Trust is the word Miranda. He'd have parties and who knows who'd be living here every weekend." Noah hefted the suitcase he held, "but enough talk about our siblings let me get Caroline settled and then we can have some lunch together, it was a very long drive."

"I'm sorry; of course you must be tired. I'll bet it was a real traffic jam from the city to here." Miranda apologized to Caro.

"It wasn't that bad." Caro smiled at her, "the scenery was well worth it."

"I'll whip up a nice lunch. You two get settled. It should be ready in about an hour."

"That'll be fine." Noah kissed his sister's cheek then started up the stairs.

Caro followed him but her eyes kept looking back at the room below. It was so...perfect. The word lingered in her mind and she knew again it was an apt description of the house. She stepped onto the second floor landing and looked out at the view of the ocean from this height. She remembered again another house similar to this one but instead of the ocean it had a magnificent view of the mountains. Where had she seen such a house? She had no idea but it was stuck in her memory from somewhere, just like Noah.

"This place is really unbelievably beautiful," she whispered then turned and walked right into Noah's chest, his arms closed around her. Startled she looked up into his intensely passionate green eyes.

Noah shook his head. "It's unbelievably beautiful with you here. My home becomes you Caroline. Maybe I knew that when I built it... at the ocean's edge...Maybe I knew that someday I would bring you here and you'd belong. You are as natural as that ocean and as mysterious as the sky above it. Can't you feel the rightness of being here...the rightness in the attraction between us?"

Caro's heart beat wildly, his words had her mind racing with images of them on a beach in a lover's embrace and it did feel real and it did feel right. She just didn't know where these images were coming from but she couldn't deny they felt real.

"Yes...I can feel it," she whispered softly.

Noah's smile beamed angelic at her words and he slowly lowered his lips to hers. "Than don't fight what you feel...explore it as you do the stars."

His lips brushed hers softly and yet she felt as if an explosion large enough to match a colliding asteroid blew her apart. He deepened the kiss and a part of her welcomed him like a long lost lover. There was definitely something between them but a noise from below made her pull back from his kiss.

They saw Miranda walking across the room below.

"Later Caroline...we'll finish this," Noah promised her with a wink and whistled happily as he walked her along to the bedrooms. His mood had completely changed from the frustration he'd been living with since meeting her. That one kiss had foretold a great deal of how she felt about him and gave him hope for their future.

"This room will be yours, it faces the ocean... I hope you like it." Noah said as he opened the door for her and walked past her into the room placing her bags on the bed.

"The room next door is mine...if you need anything just knock."

He'd pointed out to her the room further down was his sisters and that his friends, who would also be staying the weekend, would occupy the bedrooms on the first floor. "So you'll have many chaperones Caroline."

She stared at the beautiful smile he flashed at her realizing it had a tilt of happiness she hadn't seen before. It changed his whole expression from darkly intent to warm and lighthearted, and it drew her to him.

"Will I need them?" she whispered feeling dangerously playful.

"Oh you might...after what I felt in that kiss...You should count on it...and you might want to be careful Caroline," he moved closer to her as he spoke, his eyes alight with some inner glow. "Unless you're absolutely sure of what you want from me...don't be alone with me," he warned, "because I am very, very, sure of what I want from you." He held her gaze a moment longer before he lifted his own bag and went on to his room casually calling over his shoulder. "Lunch should be ready in about an hour. I'll see you downstairs."

If the wall hadn't been behind her she'd have been on the floor. Caroline stared a long time at the door that separated him from her until an image of Jon's loving face rose in her thoughts and she froze again with indecision. How could she be so fickle? How could she be so in love with Jon and even think about acting on this...Whatever 'this' was?

CHAPTER 16

Jon unlocked his apartment door but before he went in, on a hope, he walked over to Caro's and knocked softly. He knew it was foolish thinking she'd stayed home and not gone off with Noah for the weekend. A small hope he'd held onto on his long drive home. He'd stupidly pictured her waiting for him, setting himself up for an obvious disappointment.

He knocked harder but no response came from within, and none was expected. It was just his frustration that kept him knocking too hard and too long.

"Fool," he mumbled as he walked back to his empty apartment and when he pushed open the door, the silence hit him hard.

He wished he had a pet...a dog that would run to him, showering him with unconditional affection. He could use some of that right now he admitted and threw his keys onto the hall table.

The mail he'd brought up with him held nothing but bills so he placed them on his desk and stopped there, staring at the red light blinking on his answer machine.

He sat down before pressing the play button. The soft voice on the message had his heart pounding and had him leaning forward to hear every word.

"Hi Jon...I guess you're not home yet. I forgot my cell phone when we left and we just got here about an hour ago and I...I wanted to call to let you know that I...I got here okay. It's silly I know, but that's it...I just wanted to call you..."

Jon's ears listened for anything in the background that might sound like Noah in the room with her and he berated himself for even thinking about it, but he listened harder all the same.

She gave a phone number to where she was staying if he needed to contact her and he nearly reached for the phone to dial it even before her message ended.

Her voice sounded sad as she said goodbye and he froze at the sound and wondered what was going on with her and Noah, and was that sorrow a hint to her feelings?

His hand clenched the phone but he didn't pick it up. He would just have to let the weekend play out and hope in the end he could handle the outcome.

Jon concentrated on his work with intensity. It had always been his escape to create his comic world when his real one was not all he'd wanted it to be.

The time flew by and he was lost in his creative world until his stomach grumbled in protest, he needed to take a break.

He stood up and stretched the knot out of his back and decided he'd tackle next week's comic strips too

152

after a good meal and a large beer. That was his immediate plan for the future but a knock on his apartment door brought him up short. He wasn't expecting anyone.

"Hi...mind if I come in?" Nancy stood there biting her lower lip and looking like she needed a really good cry.

"No, of course not, come in," he opened the door wider.

"I don't want to intrude if you have plans... I was really on my way to see Caro but I realized too late she was away for the w-" she stopped her words not wanting to upset Jon.

"Yeah, I know." Jon looked away. It made him uneasy to think she felt sorry for him. He didn't need anyone feeling sorry for him...he could do that all by himself.

"Uh...I guess you're not in the mood for some depressing company right now. I'm sorry I'll go."

She turned to leave but Jon touched her arm. "No stay. What ever is bothering you, you need to talk about it...I'm not Caro, but I have a sympathetic ear to offer. Besides don't they say misery loves company? I should be throwing a party." He smiled ruefully and made her smile.

"Thanks Jon...I could make us some lunch," she offered shyly thinking that Jon was one fantastic guy and what the heck was wrong with Caro? How could she not see what was right before her eyes?

"Now you're talking," Jon grinned and took her elbow leading her into the kitchen, "I was just heading that way."

An hour later with a primavera salad between them a loaf of garlic bread and a bottle of white wine the world looked rosier.

"Now tell me, who made you cry today?" Jon leaned forward and tipped her chin up to him.

"A jerk and I shouldn't have let him make me cry."

"Now that, I already knew...but tell me what happened?"

Nancy nodded, feeling relaxed with Jon she pulled her feet up onto the chair and got more comfortable.

"His name is Mark Hansel. We met at the university. He's in one of my classes. It all started innocently enough...coffee after class led to an occasional movie then real dates began... Intimate restaurants on nights we didn't have school and quiet talks over dinner. He seemed sincere and I thought he genuinely cared about me...turned out he wasn't free to care about me...he was married...is married." Her feet slammed back to the ground. She stood up and paced the room.

Jon didn't interrupt her. He just let her vent.

"I saw him with his wife by accident this afternoon in Central Park. He had the nerve to call me after. Of course, now he admitted he was married and he also has three kids. Three!" She emphasized by holding up the same number of fingers and shaking her head. "I'm just grateful I hadn't taken the step I'd have regretted. We were never intimate but dating a married man goes against all I believe in. What makes a guy so selfish?" She sat down facing Jon, her expression clearly showing she expected him to enlighten her.

"Don't ask me I haven't a wife or even one kid...but if I had...I wouldn't risk them for all the beautiful women in the world...sorry."

Nancy smiled. "Thanks for the compliment...Beautiful huh? You know Jon I told Caro she should have jumped into bed with you."

Jon nearly spilled his wine and Nancy laughed. "Relax. She was seesawing and I just gave her my opinion. You two are perfect together...I don't know why she can't see it."

"Thanks for the vote but Caro can't see anything that even appears to look like a commitment."

"She said she wasn't but...has she been disappointed by some guy?"

"I've known her since she was five years old and unless it happened when she was four I'm clueless." He thought of her relationship with Mitch but he didn't think that was the cause of her fear, she was already afraid of commitment before Mitch she just didn't know it until Mitch proposed.

"Weird...really weird because she said Noah--." she cut off her own words.

Jon looked at her intently, "What? What did she say about Noah?"

"Oh nothing, its nothing..." Nancy wished she hadn't spoken her thoughts out loud. She didn't want to hurt Jon or betray Caro's trust in her.

"Please tell me," Jon asked softly.

"It's nothing really, and I shouldn't."

"Please."

His eyes pleaded with her to give him an answer to Caro's behavior and she caved.

"Okay, the other night Caro and I were discussing Noah ...and she kind of implied the reason she felt some attraction for him was...he felt sort of familiar to her."

Seeing Jon's odd expression at her words she tried to explain it better. "What I mean is ...she said she felt like she knew him even though she'd never met him before... but honestly, she wasn't comfortable with that feeling so I wouldn't worry."

"She felt like she knew him? You mean like a soul mate?"

"No! No nothing like that!" Nancy disagreed loudly. "I truly don't think that was what she meant at all." Nancy kept shaking her head but the more she tried to deny it the more it sounded like she was trying to cover it up.

Jon looked utterly miserable and Nancy wished she'd kept her big mouth shut.

*   *   *

The weather cooperated; it was a balmy fifty degrees at the beach and the night sky was clear of clouds and best of all, there were no city lights to distort the view.

The large telescopes were assembled and pointed upward, their single eyes unblinkingly watching the heavens.

Caro sat on the side of the group in a comfortably padded lounge chair watching as each new arrival to the star party set up their equipment, each telescope design was more unique than the last. She particularly liked watching Professor Delby.

Professor Delby had a wizened look about him and Noah had said he was nearly eighty. Caro thought for his age he was agile and had a very bohemian appearance. His white hair was long and pulled into a ponytail, his flower patterned shirt was something from a sixties retro store, or perhaps just from the back of his own closet. He had on a well-worn pair of jeans and a wool lined suede vest. Noah and the others treated him with utter reverence. Apparently, the man had been their professor in college and had only recently retired from the university.

When Caro listened to their conversations she understood the reverence, the man was lucid and bitingly intelligent. His views were cutting edge and he'd confidently told her he knew where undiscovered treasures of the universe could be found and he'd offered to show them to her this evening.

Caro watched him set up a large Dobsonian telescope that Noah had told her he'd personally built himself. She was very impressed with the professor.

"Having fun yet?" Noah sat down on the chair next to hers. It was nearly pitch black out except for the small, low to the ground lanterns and outdoor heaters that were placed strategically, so as not to interfere with the viewing of the night sky.

"I'm so glad you brought me this weekend. I can't believe this," she pointed to the seven magnificent telescopes set up as widows from which to view the mysteries of the universe.

"Wait 'till Professor Delby gets rolling. He'll find some of the coolest stuff."

"Why didn't you tell me this was a gathering of old college friends, beach neighbors, and one lone professor? I thought it was a more formal affair with stuffy scientists."

"Stuffy? You can't be serious. Me? Stuffy?" he leaned over pretending to raise the wick on a lantern near her and brushed his lips across hers. "Stuffy? I can show you wild if you wish it."

Caro drew back from his kiss, her eyes glowing turquoise in the firelight, his flashing like a sea on fire. They stayed like that for a heartbeat feeling the electricity of awareness flowing between them.

"Hey, Noah, Come take a look at this. I think I've got a focus on the star cluster I was telling you about." Aaron Hackenbush called down from his precarious perch upon the small ladder he'd set up next to his telescope.

Noah reluctantly looked away from Caro breaking the indefinable thread that held them. "I'll be right there," he called out as he stood up. "I'll be back…save

157

my place," he said and smiled down at her before going to see what his friend had found.

"Would you like some hot chocolate?" Miranda asked as she walked over to Caro. She was holding a thermos and two cups.

"Sure." Caro smiled at her as she sat down on the chair Noah had just vacated.

"Mmmm smells wonderful," Caro took one of the cups and held it out for the warm chocolaty brew.

"So…can I ask how long you've known my brother?" Miranda asked casually as she sipped her own steaming drink.

"Ahhh…so the drink comes with ulterior motives?" Caro replied with equal ease.

"Of course…after all he is my *little* brother." Miranda smiled at Caro. She liked her but she was afraid Noah was in deeper than he'd ever been before and big sisters had to protect their younger siblings, even if they did tower over them by several inches.

"I understand. I can't say don't worry about it because I'm not sure where we're heading…There is something between us and I'll admit Noah is ready to accept it but I'm not…not yet anyway."

"Why?"

Why? The simple word reverberated in Caro's mind. Why did he feel so familiar? Why couldn't she accept the attraction? Why did she pull back even as she reached out to him? Why did she reach out to him? Why did he come into her life after she and Jon had admitted their feelings? Why? She wished she knew.

"I don't know why…but I'm working on it," she answered honestly.

"So my brother has a good chance of getting his first broken heart?"

Caro felt the intense stare and heard the concern. "I don't know but I suppose it could be both of our hearts. Maybe even three hearts by the end of it all."

"Three?"

Caro took a deep breath and told her about Jon and all the confusion in her relationship since meeting Noah.

Miranda gave a long slow whistle, "I wouldn't want to be you Caroline but at least you're honest."

"Thanks," Caro was truly touched by Miranda's acceptance of her. Miranda didn't have to be kind to her, didn't have to understand her dilemma, but she did. And just like with Noah, she felt instantly close to her. Maybe this life was her destiny. It certainly felt right to be here, the people Noah knew, the house he'd built and of course Noah felt easy for her to be around. It all felt...perfect...so why did that worry her?

"You're welcome." Miranda tapped her cup to Caro's then drank it down, "That was just what I needed." Miranda leaned back and looked at the others. "Have you looked through Professor Delby's telescope yet?"

"No, but he did invite me to."

"You're in for a treat. He finds the most awesome stuff up there. It almost makes me want to study Astronomy...almost...but I'm more ocean savvy."

"Now I really can't wait." Caro looked over at the largest telescope on the beach and saw the professor looking into his viewer and drawing on a tablet of paper.

"What is he doing?"

"He's a really good artist too and he can capture in an instant what he sees. Sometimes he'll convert it to canvas. He has some of the wildest paintings on the walls in his home."

"You know him well?" Caro looked back at her.

"He lives down the beach and Noah and I visit him pretty often. He doesn't have family anymore. His wife died about four years ago. She was as earthy as he is and they were a perfect match but they didn't have any children...Noah and I thought that was a real shame. He would have been a great father. I think he sort of adopted Noah," she nodded in the direction of Professor Delby and Caro turned to see that Noah had wandered over to the old man.

They appeared to be discussing something the professor was drawing and Noah was looking through the telescope then looking back at the drawing and making some reference to it.

Caro was stunned by a sudden insight as she watched them together. To Noah work was very important. The details of anything he attempted would have to be worked out until they were...perfect. She could see that in his attention... no it was more than that...she could feel it about him. He'd said she would fit in his life and in his home...perfectly. That should have been a compliment, so why did that word bother her? And her reaction to the kiss they'd shared on the landing earlier, why did she feel as if she had missed him for a long time...how could you miss someone you just met?

All these intangible feelings flew through her conscious thoughts and she didn't know where they came from but she knew they had a basis in her reality and her relationship with Noah even though nothing she was thinking made the least bit of sense to her.

"Caroline."

Professor Delby had called her name and her troubling thoughts ended when she turned to look towards him. He was standing alone by his telescope calling her over to him. Noah had moved on to help his friend Dan Wilby locate something in the night sky with his telescope so Caro rose and walked over to the professor, ready for the adventure she'd been promised.

"Ready to view the past," Professor Delby asked, his eyes twinkling under his bushy white eye brows.

"The past?" Caro questioned skeptically.

"You've studied Astronomy and you don't know that what we see in our night sky is the light from things long gone?" his eyebrows shot up.

"Oh yes, of course. You mean dead stars whose light still shine in our heavens. I guess I just misunderstood," she felt completely foolish. She knew you could see the remnants of the past and the very beginnings of our universe if you looked into the deepest recesses of space. But it had been the way he'd said it that had thrown her off, it sounded personal... as if she would view her own life through the lens. Silly, but that's what she'd thought he'd meant.

"Good! Then you'll be in for a treat. I've captured the very edge of a new galaxy. Look here and you can see it...and it is way out there...nearly to the end of the visible universe. I've been charting its size and movement for a year now." He stood up from his comfortable chair and pointed for her to sit down.

Caro complied and he encouraged her to look through the lens of the telescope.

CHAPTER 17

At first Caro saw nothing but that was how it was sometimes you had to relax your eyes and look off center until the object came into view. When it did, Caro sucked in her breath.

There was a glimmer at first and then it was a perfectly shaped spiral galaxy framed in the lens, it was so like our own milky way. It was far out there and yet it was amazingly detailed.

"Wow! I *can* see it." She squealed excited at the discovery. "Has it been charted on any sky maps yet?"

"No."

"Are you going to submit it and name it?" she asked impressed with his ability.

"No."

The simple reply caused her to turn from the glorious view and look at the professor. "No? Why not? This is an amazing discovery."

"There is nothing discovered or undiscovered that is for man to lay claim to. It is for man to seek and learn from nothing more."

Caro felt the rightness in his words and it was true. Nothing created in our universe had been by man's hand so why should man take credit? Truth for sure, but that truth had not been a hindrance to man's ego to claim all he sees as his own. How fascinating to find a scientist who didn't wish to become critically acclaimed for or go down in history with his name attached to a lasting discovery.

Caro smiled up at him. "You professor are a true astronomer and a pioneer of ethics too."

"It's not anything that most don't know...I just practice it better," he smiled back at her then changed the subject, "Have you seen the constellation Orion? It is amazingly bright tonight." He set the coordinates to find the star into his telescope and then told her to look again into the lens.

Instantly, she saw the star called Orion and it really was burning with intensity. Again she was amazed at the ability of his telescope to bring such distance into detail. The clarity she was seeing reminded her of her views through the Keck telescope when she spent that one summer interning at the University of Hawaii's Institute of Astronomy.

"Your telescope is one of the best I've ever looked through," she told him honestly.

"It's good enough but look away from the lens a moment." He waited for her to look back at him, "I want you to focus your own eyes on any part of the sky. Stare at a spot in the deepest part of the heavens... look hard. What do you see?"

Caro directed her gaze where he pointed and waited, soon her vision focused and because there were no lights to deter the visibility she picked out distant stars, gas clouds and patterns of familiar constellations in the heavens.

"I see a vast array of stars, planets and constellations and the Milky Way," she said to him.

"And that Caroline is what the first ancestors of man saw as they stood and wondered what was above them. Tell me, how far have we come from that? We build bigger eyes to see the heavens with," he waved his hand at his own large telescope, "but we still basically wonder what it is above us and who created it all so precisely, was it random or designed? That question, asked since the beginning of time, is still asked today. It is a fine thread from past to future. Man exists through the creation of the universe, the creator yet unknown to us and we, after all is said and done, are but a humble work of art…a sprinkling of stardust."

"So then we don't matter?"

"Of course we do, we matter very much and as with any work of art, we have to live up to our legacy. We have to shine and strive for perfection," he lectured, but his professor's tone was tinged with kindness.

Caro looked back up at the heavens. "It's rather lonely when you think about it isn't it? Each one of us is separate…completely separate. Even when we love deeply we're still separate," the words came from her soul as she continued, "You love someone and they leave you. Like the stars dying in the sky leave their light to remind you. They leave you but you still think of them." She didn't know why she felt the need to speak these feelings but they were honest and sad and pouring forth from a place she didn't recognize.

"Yes, Caroline we are alone, each one of us separate, each one moving toward that simple act of refinement but the collisions we get into on the way shape us as well. Just as stars that collide can bring rebirth we deepen our worth as we connect and love someone. Love is the golden key that opens the way to all knowledge. Do you know the one emotion that gives us the most shine?"

Caro shook her head.

"Love Caroline...it is love. The most unselfish of all emotions when given honestly and freely and not in search of its return takes us further and closer to our creator. Look around you Caroline everything out there was created with precision and a loving hand. If we are a part of that then we are so much more than we let ourselves be, don't you think?"

Caroline wondered what it was about this Professor Delby that made her so introspective. His words invoked deeper thoughts and she felt at one with the sky above her and with everything that lived and breathed as she never had before. So why in the midst of all this understanding did she still fear to love? Why the undeniable worry that no matter how much she cared about the man she loved he would leave her alone...utterly and completely alone? Of course that had never happened to her and she'd never told this feeling to anyone, not even Jon, but she'd always known that was the root cause of her fear of commitment.

"Caroline?"

Noah's deep voice broke into her introspection and she turned to find him standing next to Professor Delby. She was sorry he had chosen that moment to interrupt, she'd felt she'd been close to discovering some truth about herself.

"What fascinating find have you shown Caroline?" he asked the professor.

"Me? I have no fascinating finds Noah. I'm just a star watcher like you," The Professor smiled and held his hand out to Caro to help her up, "I think Noah feels I've monopolized enough of your time."

"That's not true." Noah looked at Caroline and shook his head, "I know you have a way of making a person see the heavens clearer and I'm sure Caroline loved seeing it."

Caro turned to the professor, "I did and you sure do...Professor, I can't thank you enough for what you've helped me discover."

"No need for thanks. I never show anyone anything they didn't already have the ability to see." He smiled at her then sat down, looked into the lens of his telescope, and completely tuned them out.

Noah took her arm. "He's like that, very absorbed in his work. We'll check back with him later...would you like something to eat? Miranda has a buffet supper set up in the house and it'll be winding down out here in the next hour."

"I guess I am hungry...Noah?"

"Yes?" he turned to her and easily gave her his full attention. She stood in a pool of moonlight with a backdrop of midnight sky and ocean. The effect was hypnotizing, he barely heard her words.

"I can't thank you enough for invit-" Caro began but didn't finish because Noah gently pulled her to him.

"Don't thank me Caroline...My motives were not for your scientific education. I wanted to have you to myself this weekend. I'd hoped we could discover some common ground to build a relationship between us."

Was there ever any 'us'? Caro thought back to her discussion with the professor. If the door to commitment was learning to accept that we were ultimately alone then maybe she needed to accept it. And maybe it was time to open that door.

"I'll try to Noah…I'll really try to."

His face lit up with a boyish grin just before he kissed her.

Noah led her into the dinning room from the sliding glass doors that led from the beach to the house.

Caro took a moment to savor the delicious aromas filling the room before she surveyed the unbelievable amount of food displayed. On a large side board was a veritable profusion of epicurean delights. Sliced roast beef nestled along side a tenderly done turkey breast, thinly sliced and steaming from the oven and next to that was a temptingly glazed ham. There was salmon and fresh tuna arranged upon a bed of lettuce and cut into tantalizing portions next to an array of vegetables of every imagined kind both streamed and sauced to complete the menu.

The dining room table held no less than four kinds of what appeared to be freshly baked breads and in the center of the table sat two large tossed salads in huge bowls with several kinds of dressings arranged in serving cups by each bowl.

"You can't tell me that Miranda did this all by herself." Caro turned to Noah.

"Of course not, although she is a great cook, some dishes were brought by Dan's wife and Aaron's and some I must admit were delivered from a local caterer. However, the desserts, when we get to that, are all Miranda's. She loves to bake and enjoys when we have these get-togethers because it gives her a reason to pull out all the stops and bake up a storm… as you'll soon find out."

"I don't think I'll have room for dessert," Caro admitted as she took a plate and began filling it with small portion of everything.

"Believe me no matter how full you are when you see her cakes and pies not to mention the cookies and brownies and-"

"Stop! Please don't say any more or I'll get full just listening," she laughed and waited for Noah to finish making his own plate before they sat down at the table and both silently agreed to avoid the bread and salad to save room for dessert after all.
"Ah! My first arrivals," Miranda smiled at them as she carried a large pan of lasagna out from the kitchen.

"Oh my, are you trying to kill me?' Caro asked sniffing the air and closing her eyes, "That is my absolute favorite meal," she said with reverence.

Miranda laughed. "Well Dan's wife is from Sicily and her family recipe is to die for. I'll cut you a piece."

"No, I shouldn't."

Miranda passed by her on the way to the side board and the smell of the home made dish did her in.

"Okay, maybe just a teeny, tiny portion."

Miranda cut two servings, a bit more than tiny, and gave one to her and one to Noah. Then she made herself a plate and sat down to join them.

They were only half way through their meal when the rest of the party started to enter.

Dan was grumbling about the smell of the delicious food breaking into his concentration.

"I'm sure you'll get over the disappointment when you taste this stuff," Lillian, Dan's wife, patted his arm with exaggerated sympathy.

"You had to make the Lasagna didn't you?" He shook his head and piled a heaping portion of it onto a plate.

Aaron was behind him and complained he wasn't leaving enough for him 'because he loved Lily's lasagna too.'

Aaron's wife, Helen, scolded him that he didn't need any and patted his belly for emphasis and laughed when her husband piled a double helping onto her plate and said he'd just share some of hers.

The last to give up the watch was Professor Delby. He strolled casually in and as Caro might have guessed he passed up anything of the meat variety and doubled up on all the vegetables and fish.

Lily looked over at the professor and then went into the kitchen coming back out with a small casserole dish which she placed before him and lifted the lid.

The Professors eyes lit up with gratitude.

"Ah Lily" he breathed in the steaming fragrance from the dish, "Vegetable lasagna…are you sure I can't convince you to leave Dan? I could make you very happy."

"Sorry Professor, although it's tempting, especially after he forgot our anniversary last month, but I've decided he needs me more. You're already the best you can be but Dan…well…he needs a lot of work." She looked at her husband with comical sympathy and he scoffed.

"I need work? Who lost the car keys and we found them three days later in the freezer? Not me. Not Dan," he nodded and then took a bite of garlic bread that Lily had also made.

"You see professor he has no sense of discretion," Lily sadly shook her head and as she passed her husband she playfully swatted his.

The good-natured humor and easy friendship was evident among them and Caro was glad to be a part of it. She really felt welcomed and not the least bit uncomfortable. If she did decide she could love Noah this would not be a difficult life to live. These people made her laugh. They put her at ease and she felt natural around them...but then she thought of Jon and Nancy and their mutual friends. Jon's cartoonist colleagues, Mark and Divinia Russell and Tom and Rachel Kutchinski they made her feel just as comfortable but in a different way, a different lifestyle perhaps, but just as natural. The life she would lead with either man wouldn't be difficult but picking which man ...and committing to that love...that was the difficult part.

CHAPTER 18

Saturday morning dawned colder than the day before and there was even a threat of a nor'easter coming in by the evening. Hearing the weather report over the radio, the two other couples, Dan and Lillian and Aaron and Helen decided to head home early. After they finished breakfast Dan and Aaron went outside to dismantle their equipment while Lillian and Helen went to pack.

Professor Delby lingered over his coffee and asked if Noah and Caroline were planning to leave too?

"No, we're here for the whole weekend," Noah told him.

"Then if you have no other plans, why don't you both come over for dinner. It'll be a fine night for storm viewing," he nodded to Noah.

"We'd love to."

Noah accepted for them both and Caro couldn't find a way to graciously back out. She absolutely hated storms and really wished they could leave early too, but Noah hadn't notice her reticence or her worried eyes.

"You're going to love Professor Delby's viewing room. He had it built into his attic." Noah told her expecting her to be impressed by it.

"Really, that's wonderful...I can't wait to see it...but...don't you think we might have to evacuate the beach area? I mean, what if the approaching storm worsens?" Caro smiled weakly trying hard to keep the fear from her voice and apparently succeeding where Noah was concerned.

Noah thought she wanted to be reassured it was safe to stay so he brushed away her concerns, "This is typical winter weather for us. It's nothing we aren't used to," he assured her with his words but his attention was drawn to something outside the window.

"Uh, oh...I think I'd better go lend Dan a hand, he seems to be having a problem getting his telescope apart."

Noah stood up reaching for his coat and Professor Delby, who also noticed Dan's problem, said he'd go with him.

When the door closed behind them Caro found herself at the table with Miranda, the only one who *had* noticed her reaction to the impending weather.

Caro stared out the window. The darkening sky gave her chills even in the toasty warm kitchen. She hated storms. Any other day, she'd be very curious to see Professor Delby's home but today she wasn't thrilled. Why would anyone want to be on the beach during a possible nor'easter? Noah didn't seem the least bit worried about it but everyone else was leaving, even Miranda had said she'd be leaving this afternoon.

Caro wished Jon were here with her, he would understand. He would take her home. She wanted very badly to call him and hear his voice, she needed to hear his voice but she'd called both his home and cell phone yesterday and left a message with the number here and he hadn't called her.

"More coffee," Miranda asked as she refilled her own cup.

"No thanks. It's delicious but I've had three cups already." Caro picked up her cup and took it over to the sink to rinse it.

"Maybe that's why you're a tad shaky about this storm?"

Caro looked back at Miranda seeing her concern and shrugged, "No, it's not the coffee…I wish I could say it was or that this is an isolated feeling but I've always hated storms."

"I understand. Everyone has something they fear but why didn't you just tell Noah? He'd understand. I know he'd drive back today if he knew you were worried."

"No, I can't. I don't want to ruin the weekend because of a little rain and wind…and some silly thunder and lightening," she looked back out at the sky and her voice grew weaker with each word.

"You really are afraid of storms."

Caro nodded, "Terrified. I don't know why it affects me like this. I shouldn't let it. I'm a big girl not a little kid." She tried to sound brave but inside she knew she wouldn't want to step outside once it started. She could manage well enough if she stayed inside. Jon had always helped her get through a storm from the very first day he'd figured out how she felt about them, back in grade school. He was there for her and even made her laugh when a storm brewed outside. He'd make her play Charades or a card game and before you knew it the storm had passed.

She really missed him right now. She closed her eyes and admitted how much she needed him…and she loved him.

*   *   *

Jon watched the dark clouds gathering outside his window. He'd caught the weather report earlier and knew the city was going to get a downpour but the brunt of the storm was going to hit some where along the coast of Long Island.

He wondered if he should call Caro. He knew how petrified she was of storms. He hoped she was heading home but that could be worse if they were driving in a downpour. Would Noah understand her fear and keep her safe, he hoped so. That thought chilled him, what had he just wished for?

Jon shut down the graphic image of Noah consoling Caro. As his hand automatically went to the phone and dialed the number he'd memorized. He didn't know what hotel she was staying at because she'd only left him a number and as it rang he wished she'd remembered to bring her cell phone. He waited for the hotel's front desk clerk to answer.

"Hello." A deep masculine voice came over the line and Jon froze. Was that Noah? Had Caro given him the direct number to her room and was Noah sharing that room with her?

"Hello?" The voice rose demanding the party answer.

Jon hung up the phone. He felt stupid for not asking for Caro but if she were there with Noah what would he say to her? "Are you okay? Can I drive there and bring you home?" Not likely, fool! And that's what he was, a fool. She was going to be just fine with Mr. Soul Mate. He was the one in need of solace today not Caro.

He grabbed his coat from the closet and decided he needed crowds of people around him; the silence of the apartment was killing him.

        *   *   *

"Who was that?" Caro asked hoping it was Professor Delby canceling the evening but no such luck Noah said it was just a wrong number.

She slowly buttoned up her down parka and pulled her hood tighter around her face but she was shivering uncontrollably. Noah still hadn't noticed her reluctance to go out in the storm. He was busy gathering some charts he had wanted to show the Professor. She waited by the door.

"I've got everything I need," he said wrapping a plastic tarp around the charts.

A brilliant flash of lightening lit up the night sky when he opened the door, "Wow! Did you see that? This is going to be a great storm. Come on," he yelled and ran out the door thinking she was sprinting along right behind him.

Caro watched from the door as he got about three feet away and then she took a deep breath, closed her eyes, and ran after him. She didn't open them again until she ran right into his back.

"Hey?" he laughed and turned around to her putting his arm around her shoulders and guided her through the driving rain to Professor Delby's house that was a half a block away.

Noah knocked on the door and Caro plastered herself to his side trying to get as far under the portico as possible. Noah finally looked down at her.

The rain dripped from her hair where it hung in her eyes and her eyes were wide pools of worry. No not worry, he suddenly realized but pure fear.

"Hey, it's only a storm...it'll pass."

Caro shook her head but when she opened her mouth to reply a loud crack of thunder had her throwing herself into his arms instead.

That was how Professor Delby found them when he opened his door.

"Come in…you two could drown out there," he smiled at the young couple and opened the door wider. "It's a powerful storm tonight, hey Noah?" he asked as he looked out his doorway at the threatening weather then he closed the door locking it against the strong wind before turning to his guests. "Go on into the living room, I have a fire roaring and Betsy made some warm cider. We'll get rid of that winter chill in no time."

The house was big and old, but well kept. The furniture was a mixture of antique and contemporary that worked well together. The main room where the Professor led them was warmly lit from the fire's glow and a few low lighting lamps. Several comfortable chairs were scattered about the room, two extremely comfortable looking sofas faced each other near the fireplace.

An older woman was setting out platters on a long table across the room and she turned to them when they entered.

"Good evening Noah."

"Good evening Betsy. I'd like you to meet Caroline," he turned to Caro and said, "Betsy is Professor Delby's Housekeeper."

"Nice to meet you dear," Betsy stepped closer and immediately noticed Caroline was shivering, "You're positively wet and cold to the core, that won't do. You come along with me. I'll show you where the powder room is and you can dry off before you catch a cold."

Caro was grateful to the woman, "Thank you. I'd like that."

She followed Betsy up the stairs and along a wide hallway. Caro couldn't help looking at all the paintings that were displayed on the walls of the hallway. They were vivid displays of nebulas, supernovas, star clusters, planets, and all of them were as three-dimensional as a painting could get. Caro was awed by the color and brilliance of scope the artist used, and she knew from her conversation with Miranda that the artist was Professor Delby.

"He's very good isn't he?" Caro said as she stopped by a particularly breathtaking depiction of the constellation Cygnus, the swan. Each star in the constellation was captured perfectly in form and brightness.

Betsy walked over to her and gazed at the painting. "Yes, Professor Delby has vision. He is very good at seeing all the depth and colors of a subject."

"He's very talented," Caro agreed as she scanned the pictures along his walls, "His wife...was she into astronomy too?" she asked.

"Yes and no."

Caro looked curiously at Betsy waiting for her to elaborate.

"She was more of an Astrologer. She believed in the ancient teachings of the planets and stars as maps for human personality and circumstances."

"That must have been some relationship. Most Astronomers don't believe in Astrology."

"No, not all do, but Professor Delby is special. I don't know how much he believed in the teachings of ancient Astrology but he certainly believed in Natalie. She was very good at charting the skies and predicting changes in the human element in the world. Come over here," Betsy led her down to the end of the hall, "This painting was a tribute to her. When she died, Professor Delby spent days painstakingly charting the sky, he captured it exactly as it was on the last day of her life. He said he'd painted it so he would always have her with him. It gave me chills when he first hung it there but, after a time, I came to feel comforted by it too."

Caro looked at the planets in perfect alignment and a chill ran up her spine, she didn't know much about astrology but something in the alignment felt like an ending and a beginning, how very odd to feel that, she thought.

"It must have been a very difficult time for him. Losing the one you love is a life altering moment, possibly even a life ending one, even if you continue to live." She knew in the darkest secret places in her soul that she truly feared that kind of loss.

Footsteps down the hall made her turn from the painting. Noah was walking towards them.

"I started worrying about you," he said to Caro.

"I got side tracked by these paintings and Betsy was telling me all about them."

Betsy smiled at Noah, "You know I'm proud of them. I couldn't help it."

"I understand. The Professor is a talented artist." Noah stopped in front of a wild night sky showered in starlight and swirling gases. It drew him in and made him feel as if he'd stepped out into the recesses of deep space.

He ran a finger along the course of a fine shooting star and admitted, "I once tried to get him to give a showing at the university but he wouldn't. He prefers to keep his talents locked up here where only he and a chosen few can enjoy them."

"He doesn't share much with the world. You're very lucky he lets you in." Betsy advised him softly.

"Yes I am…very lucky," Noah's smile was soft then he looked away from the painting, "Well enough of this we've left him alone and that isn't very nice."

"If you show Caroline where to freshen up, I'll go back down and have dinner set out by the time you both come down."

"Sure," Noah agreed and he directed Caro to a door at the end of the hallway.

He waited for her in a small study that faced the ocean and when she walked in to the room a few moments later he told her to take a look at a book he was holding.

"What is it?" She asked and looked over his shoulder at the rather odd looking binding of the book and read the title out loud, "The Universe We Never See."

Noah handed the book to her and she opened it up. The first page held a dedication, it said 'To Natalie, my love and my light. My conscience is clear as you hold in your hand my promise to fulfill your every wish...but of course in my way.'

Caro flipped through the book and saw that the paintings that hung on the walls in his home were captured on the pages.

"I don't understand? Did Professor Delby have his work published?"

"No. He had a friend who was a professor in journalism at the college make this one copy. His wife had wanted him to show his genius to the world but this was the only concession he could make. He had his paintings photographed and bound in this book just for her and He gave it to her the Christmas before she died. He was glad he'd given her that token and he keeps it here and looks at it every night. He says it's his connection to her. Isn't that beautiful?"

"I think it's sad," Caro touched the inscription.

"Sad?" Noah looked at her.

"Yes. He loved her so much and now he has to finish his life without her," Caro closed the book and handed it back to Noah, "Love can devastate and rip you apart and leave you utterly alone."

Noah was baffled by her unromantic response, "I'm not so sure Professor Delby would agree. Love can make your days sharper and brighter. And even after decades apart those days will shine through all the days of your life. Yes, he misses her but he would never have forfeited his time with her even knowing she would go first. She was his soul mate and she lives with him still in every beat his heart takes." Noah spoke of Professor Delby but somehow he felt he was telling her something she needed to know…and he couldn't say why, but he knew it was important that she understand.

Caro felt uncomfortable with the subject and unreasonably angry with Noah. "Maybe, you're right. I wouldn't know," she murmured, "I think we should go back down stairs Betsy said she was going to set the dinner out. We shouldn't make her wait for us," she turned to walk out of the room but Noah touched her arm and she looked back at him.

"Caro don't run from love. It would be the biggest mistake you could make in your life."

"I'm not running from love," she tried to sound convincing but her voice wavered with the last word. She didn't want to continue this discussion. "We really should go back down."

Noah stared deeply into her eyes and wished he could see how she saw him. Understand why she was avoiding what was between them? He wanted to probe into what she'd just said but she was right they did need to go back downstairs. He put the book down on the desk and shrugged, "You're right." He held his hand out to her and waited until she placed her hand in his.

"Do you feel better?" Professor Delby asked Caroline when she and Noah returned to the parlor, at her nod he smiled, "Good! Then both of you come sit by the fire." They sat down on the comfortable couch facing the fireplace and Betsy brought them each a glass of warm cider.

"You can't be too careful," the professor cautioned, "that cold rain gets into the bones. I know at my age I don't even venture out on nights like this…but I do like to watch them from inside," he nodded to the dark clouds beyond his sliding glass doors that led out to the beach.

The ocean didn't seem far enough away, Caro thought even as she looked at it from her cozy vantage point. In the last light of sunset, she watched the waves tumble and roil, crashing with a vengeance against the shore and she quietly admitted, "It does have a mesmerizing effect but are you sure we shouldn't have left for higher ground?" She was afraid that the storm could harm her.

Noah caught the agitation in her voice and experienced something like Déjà vu. He could feel her fear and it felt as if he should know its origin. He felt certain of that but he couldn't fathom why he would. He put his arm around her to comfort and protect her. "Don't fear the storm Caroline. I promise you'll be safe here. It looks a lot worse than it is. Trust me, I'll protect you," he turned her face to his and tried to reassure her with his presence.

Caro calmed at his words but something about the moment triggered a feeling that her fear and his comforting her had happened before. Rationally, it couldn't have. They'd never been together in a storm before, but she couldn't convince herself she wasn't reliving a moment.

A loud clap of thunder rumbled through the house and their eyes locked on each other as a foggy memory began to form between them but hovered just beyond their grasp of recollection.

"You're sheltered from the storm here, Caroline, you've no need to fear it," The Professor promised as he turned from the window.

His words sliced through the odd moment and Caro and Noah both blinked and looked up at him. What had he just said? They didn't know but the Professor was motioning for them to follow him and they stood up while a bit of the fogginess still lingered around them.

"I believe everything is set out for our meal so let's leave the storm to brew a bit and enjoy the fine cuisine of my lovely cook," The Professor winked at Betsy.

Noah dropped his arm from Caro's shoulder and the strange connection was broken as they followed the Professor into the dinning room.

CHAPTER 19

"After dinner we can show Caroline my observations deck." Professor Delby said as he passed a large serving bowl steaming with mashed potatoes to Noah.

"I'm sure we won't see much tonight with all the cloud cover," Caro said taking the bowl from Noah realizing she felt truly disappointed at that.

"You may be surprised what we can see Caroline," the Professor said as he passed her a plate of mouthwatering, gravy smothered, pork chops, Betsy had made just for them.

"Weather is just as fascinating as the stars. As a matter of fact," he continued as he picked up another bowl and scooped out a large serving of creamed spinach onto his plate, "when we look out on a clear night into the galaxies we are viewing areas of space that are wrought with storms. Massive gas storms, violent windstorms can all be viewed in our lenses," he spoke in his professional teacher of Astronomy voice and his guests suddenly became his students. "Oh yes," he smiled at them seeing he had their attention and nodded, "Weather is fascinating through a telescope."

Caro watched the light in his eyes as he spoke of the universe and she gazed beyond him at the dimly lit walls. Even in this low light she could see there were more paintings there. Paintings he'd created.

The Professor's soothing voice, the candlelight, and Noah's solid presence next to her safely cocooned her and she was less afraid of the storm pelting the beach now. Surprisingly, she was even beginning to feel excitement for the evening to come, storm watching and all.

Caro wasn't disappointed. All she'd imagined about Professor Delby's observation telescope was true. It was massive; it could rival a good university telescope anytime. There was a retractable skylight in his attic's ceiling but tonight the rain obliterated any hope of seeing through it so Professor Delby had the telescope aimed out the side doors of the attic. His attic room had a widow's walk that extended out from the house. He told Caro it was called a widows walk because, in the early 1800's when these houses were built, sailor's wives would walk out on these attic porches on stormy days watching for their husbands to return safely to them but many times they didn't, and so these wooden structures received their name.

In Professor Delby's house his widow's walk was fitted out to accommodate his observatory. It had an over hanging roof that extended beyond the walk and retracted when the weather was nice. It was used for viewing in all weather, even on stormy nights such as tonight.

The room, other than the imposing telescope, was haphazardly furnished almost as an after thought to human comfort. There was of course the observation chair that was uniquely designed for the professor and then there was an odd array of oversized beanbags and low coffee tables for any friends who may come to visit. There was a desk with a computer next to a wall full of file cabinets and shelves that took up the other half of the large room.

Caro threw her self into one of the velour covered beanbag chairs and wiggled her body into it until its shape hugged hers perfectly, making it a very uniquely comfortable chair.

She snuggled deeper and smiled remembering how she had begged for one of these as a child. Her Mom thought it would be bad for her posture but her Dad had bought her one that same year for her birthday, along with a purple lava lamp. She had been all of eight years old but the memory was still warm and fuzzy to her.

She glanced at Noah and noticed he'd taken a seat by the desk in the typical lumbar support computer chair. He wouldn't throw himself into a contortion to fit into the beanbag chair but she knew that Jon would have, not only because he had loved her chair when they were kids but because even now all grown up he still knew how to enjoy things ...even silly things. Could Noah enjoy silly things? She wasn't sure he could.

"Caroline would you like to go first?" The professor broke into her comparisons of the two men in her life and she turned to him and smiled.

"Actually Professor, I'm enjoying watching the rain on your skylight right now and I'm really comfortable ...let Noah have first crack," she offered and sipped the soda she'd brought up with her.

Noah glanced at her and shook his head, "You know that chair can ruin your posture." She nearly spit out her soda, He actually sounded like her mother! Her eyes were wide as saucers as she watched him walk across the room towards the telescope.

185

"I've positioned it where a good break in the clouds shows the area I wanted you to note for me. My eyes are not as sharp as I'd like anymore but I think I see some wobble there. I'd like you to confirm it for me."

The Professor was using his computer to adjust his telescope for Noah. Noah took a pad and pencil from the desk ready to notate his observations.

All very proper, Caro thought as she watched him, so organized, so factual, so *perfect.*

In that instant, she realized she didn't always like perfect. She liked to look at things in many ways, study it emotionally and then define its properties. She even liked the mythical stories of the constellations sometimes more than the cold hard facts of each stars properties.

Closing her eyes she was lulled into a light sleep by the low sounds of their voices and as she drew on what they discussed she fell into a daydream.

The stars in the heavens and man's fascination with them wove into Caro's dream. She become a part of it all, knew for certain that she had all the answers to every mind breaking question man asked. She should have been happy there but she wasn't because she knew she was being watched. She felt him but couldn't see him and the frustration of his being there but not letting her see him annoyed her because she had something to tell him, something they needed to talk about.

He was there in the shadows of the heavens and she was going to confront him but the sky around her changed, darkened and lightening began to spark. She stood before a harsh white light and entities that she could not see determined her fate. They were telling her she had to leave and the very air around her became a violent lightning storm and the last thing Caro saw before she woke up with a start was Noah's face in the center of those bright light beings that had sent her out into the cold, harsh storm.

It must have only been minutes that she had dozed but the dream had been so intense that she felt it had lasted hours. What had the dream meant? That Noah confused her she understood but what exactly was her subconscious trying to tell her?

"Your turn Caroline," Noah's deep voice drew her attention to him. For perhaps the millionth time since meeting him, she wondered why he felt so familiar, was there a past life between them? She tried to shake it off as ridiculous but it didn't feel impossible anymore. She looked at him as he waved her over.

"You should come see this Caroline, you won't want to miss this," Noah urged her to look through the lens.

"All right, I'll take my turn."

Caro easily lifted out of the low chair and walked over to the telescope prepared to be impressed all over again by Professor Delby and she wasn't disappointed.

By the evenings end, she had been more than impressed and she had been forever changed. Storms would no longer frighten her in quite the same way as before, but Noah was another story.

The storm had subsided and there was a full moon reflecting off the ocean as they walked back to Noah's house.

"Did you enjoy the evening, Caroline?"

"Yes I did, very much. Professor Delby is a marvelous teacher."

Caro's voice was nearly lost with the roar of the waves but he heard her and turned her to face him.

"I'm glad you liked Professor Delby but have you decided what you feel for me?"

His desire telegraphed instinctively along her nerve endings straight to her heart.

Caro could fall into his arms and welcome his kiss but her heart, although warmed, did not melt. She couldn't define it but something stopped her from moving closer.

Noah saw her reluctance, "You don't have to answer," he sighed and changed the subject. "Did you bring your bathing suit?" he asked nonchalantly.

Caro had forgotten about the hot tub but she had brought her suit and wondered if that had been a foolish thing to do.

"Yes, I did," she murmured casually, not looking his way as they walked.

"Good," he said matter-of-factly but she could have sworn she felt tension in the arm that was draped over her shoulder.

"It will be very relaxing to soak away the chill from the night. Will you join me?"

"I'll think about it."

Caro sighed as she sank lower into the hot tub. It was heavenly to immerse herself in the warm bubbling water. Noah had been right, it did completely relax her.

Noah sat across studying her angelic expression. "Feels wonderful, doesn't it?" he asked.

"Mmmm," the contended sound escaped her lips. Her eyes were closed and she enjoyed the pulse of the jets against her lower back.

Noah slid closer to her watching the light from the candles play across her lovely features. She was breathtakingly beautiful and he knew, from the moment he'd met her, they were meant to be together forever.

Noah leaned over and kissed her softly.

Caro responded slowly. Her hand moved up his chest and drew him closer to her. She felt pliant and warm in the heated water and her mind was in a half dream state. She let feelings guide her as she imagined herself married to Noah. She was welcoming her husband's kiss after a long day at work now that they were home in their Mountain view house and relaxing in the hot tub that was just off their bedroom.

Noah caressed her waist under the water and moved her closer to him as he deepened the kiss.

Caro was under the spell of her imagination; desire welled up inside her. She moaned as his kiss became bolder. It felt natural to be in his arms...he was her husband- No, he wasn't!

Her imagination screeched to a halt as she realized she was welcoming his body with hers and she wasn't nearly ready for that. She moved her hand between them and his eyes opened.

He stared questioningly at her but she couldn't rationalize her actions in words, she could only shake her head but it was enough to effectively end the moment.

Noah moved back but asked her, "What are you afraid of Caroline? You can't tell me you don't feel how incredibly right this is between us." His searching eyes waited for her to admit the truth of his words.

"That's exactly what I'm afraid of," she admitted in a soft voice.

Her words gave him hope but her next words dashed that hope.

"I think I'd better call it a night," she murmured and quickly climbed out of the hot tub grabbing a large thick yellow towel to wrap around her red bikini clad torso.

Noah shook his head and leaned his arms along the side of the hot tub, he wouldn't run after her.

"Caroline someday you will have to stop running from me."

"I'm not running." She looked over her shoulder at him and realized she was nearly out of the room.

"No? Then you're walking very fast."

She shrugged, "I just don't think I know you well enough--"

Noah quickly climbed out of the hot tub. The sight of his wet muscular body cut off her words.

"Oh, you know me...Caroline don't deny that! If you're still afraid to go further I understand, but don't lie," He stopped in front of her, "You *know* me," his eyes were burning with intensity, making it impossible for her to look away.

"Yes, somehow I do," Caro whispered, in some as yet untapped knowledge of what might have been between them she did know him, "Alright, I admit I feel it but I also feel confused and angry about it and I don't know why."

"Maybe it's because you've been so good at avoiding commitment. Don't you think you're angry that this time it won't be easy to do that?" His words were soft not condemning.

Caro had to admit on some level what he said made sense. She had been afraid of commitment for so long it could very well be the reason feeling connected to him made her angry.

Noah watched his words register.

She looked at him curiously as he bent down and this time the kiss was a release of emotions so powerful he could feel her going weak in his arms. When her hands rose between them it was to move tentatively along his shoulders making him shiver with need because she was drawing him closer and deepening the kiss on her own.

   *   *   *

Jonathon signed his name with a bold stroke on the last panel of his cartoon. He sat back and studied his work. It was for the Christmas week edition and even though his heart wasn't in a festive mood he tried not to let it affect his work. He gave the strip a critical once over.

In the strip, Cal and Ivy were best friends but every reader knew that Cal loved Ivy and that Ivy didn't suspect it. Ivy was oblivious to Cal's affections much the same as Caro had been oblivious to Jon's, until recently.

Jon knew his comic strip reflected his own life and relationship with Caro. It always had, and he felt the poignancy of it even more as he waited for her to come home from her weekend with Noah, for her to come home to him.

His eyes followed the flow of the cartoon. Cal and Ivy were sitting across the aisle from each other, sitting with their parents at midnight mass on Christmas Eve.

Cal was glancing sideways at Ivy and in an imagination bubble he was fantasizing about them being together in some future Christmas a whole decade ahead.

Ivy glanced at Cal too but her imagination bubble depicted them outside playing in the newly falling snow instead of listening to the sermon.

They both smiled secretively at each other and in unison whispered 'Merry Christmas'.

In that small cartoon a lot was said and it clearly defined the rift between him and Caro. She lived in the now, never wanting to see the future, and he constantly dreamed of her in hopes of a commitment for tomorrow.

Didn't someone say tomorrow never came? Jon snorted, boy were they ever right!

He tossed the ink pen onto his desk, picked up the strip and stuffed it into a large envelope.

He could deliver it to the newspaper office today but he wanted to wait for Caro.

He turned the envelope over in his hands as he realized again how the little cartoon pretty much summed up his life.

Would he go on thinking of them together, as in married, and would Caro take him a day at a time forever? Or worse, could this weekend have suddenly made her all for a commitment, a commitment with Noah? He nearly crumbled the envelope he held in his hands at the thought.

"Where was she?" Jon glanced at his watch. It was already Sunday afternoon and she'd said she'd be home by now. He walked to his window and looked out. It had turned bitterly cold this morning after yesterday's rain had turned to snow. There were few cars moving below. He looked up and down the length of the block as far as he could see but didn't spot any familiar figure walking on the sidewalk below.

"Could she have decided to stay longer with Noah?" he didn't really look forward to confronting her about his call yesterday. He had almost convinced himself he'd dialed a wrong number and how could he be sure it was Noah's voice when he'd only met him once. He could have misdialed...but he knew he hadn't.

Aside from wondering where Noah had spent his nights this weekend, he also couldn't forget what Nancy had said to him...that Caro admitted Noah seemed familiar to her. What did that mean anyway? Familiar...was she imagining him as her soul mate?

Disgusted with his thoughts, Jon walked away from the window, afraid he'd already lost her and there wasn't anything he could do about it.

They couldn't go back to being just friends. After having come so close to having it all with her it would actually kill his spirit if he had to accept less than love from her, and he knew he wouldn't do it.

192

This weekend was the end, one-way or another, this was the final act in their relationship.

It either went forward towards a commitment or they went their separate ways.

CHAPTER 20

Noah carried her bag and walked behind her up to her apartment.

On the drive home she wouldn't talk about the weekend or answer when he spoke of commitment. Last night had only been the beginning of breaking through her fears.

They hadn't made love but they'd talked until nearly dawn and then fell asleep wrapped in each other's arms.

She promised to tell Jonathon today that she would be seeing Noah exclusively, and tonight she would be his alone.

Noah dropped her bag just inside her apartment and pulled her close to him. He tilted her face up to his, "If I have to leave at least give me something to dream on," he lowered his lips to hers and she willingly met them with her own. He wanted to draw her into himself, absorb all that she was. He didn't want to let her go and too soon she ended the kiss.

"You have to go Noah. I have to unpack and I really need to talk with Jon."

"I know…I understand," he pulled her with him to the door and she walked him out into the hallway.

"I'll pick you up at six, be ready," he turned to go but instead turned back and pulled her into his arms, "I love you."

She didn't answer in kind so he kissed her in a way that left no doubt how much he loved her.

Caro stared at him. Their eyes locked and lost in each other, neither heard the apartment door opening down the hall or realized their tender moment was being observed.

Noah took the stairs two at a time leaping down them and whistling as he headed out. Caro wanted to follow but hesitated.

A noise to her left had her turn and she saw Jonathan. He was leaning against the wall just outside his apartment. From his vantage point and his expression she knew he'd seen it all.

"Hi!" she said weakly and watched as he took a deep breath before he moved to walk over to her.

"How was your weekend?" he nodded towards the now empty landing where Noah had stood only a moment before kissing her. "I'm guessing it went well?" he offered casually but his eyes were slits of anger.

"Jon, I know what you saw-"

"Please Caro don't…you weren't pushing him away."

"No, I wasn't but-."

"Are you saying you still don't know what you want?" This time the disbelief in his voice was apparent.

Caro stared at him in shock; she had never seen Jon jealous or angry, really angry, at her!

"Caro I'm not a puppy waiting here for your meager affections. I can't do this anymore. It's obvious there's something between you and Noah, and I...I can't wait for the scraps of love you might toss me when your here...and wonder what you're doing when you're with him," his eyes were intense. "Maybe it's time to let this go."

She stared at him uncomprehendingly.

He shook his head, "It's time for *me* to go," and without any further explanation he walked back towards his apartment.

"Wait! Jon, what are you talking about? What do you mean go? Go where?"

Losing Jon was something she didn't want, not at all. She admitted she felt like she did belong with Noah this weekend but she'd never doubted what she felt for Jon. She loved Jonathon and needed him in her life. Noah confused her and there was something deep within her that she needed to unearth but she couldn't lose Jon from her life.

Everything was wrong and no matter what Noah made her feel she couldn't let go of Jon. He was her best friend.

But how could she really stop him?

Lately, she'd felt like a puppet following some destiny she didn't want, having no idea what it was or how to change it.

The sound of Jon's apartment door as it slammed shut sounded like a death knell.

She heard the bolt slide into place and she walked over to his door.

She tried to turn the knob but the door was locked. She bit her lip in indecision then dug in her bag for the key he'd given her.

When she entered the living room was empty. She heard a noise in the kitchen and walked softly across the floor.

She saw him, his back was to her, and he was staring out the kitchen window.

"Jon?" she called quietly and saw his shoulders tense.

"You shouldn't have come over, Caro. I don't really feel like talking to you." He didn't turn around.

"Would you listen to me?"

"No." the one word was spoken quietly.

"You won't listen to me."

"I'm sorry Caro. I can't do this anymore."

He turned and walked past her into his living room.

She followed.

"Please Jon, you know I love you. I do. I just…. I just…I'm so confused about Noah. I hate that I feel this pull and I don't want to hurt anyone. Not you, never you. You've been my best friend for forever. I couldn't live without-"

Jon turned around suddenly, the pain in his eyes cut off her words. "Your soul mate, or is that Noah?" at Caro's stunned silence he continued," You say you can't live without me but you mean it as a friend. And I can't live with you as a friend, not anymore. It would kill me to have to and that's why I'm leaving. You don't have to worry about making a decision any more Caro, because I've made one."

"You're leaving?"

He nodded.

"Please don't."

He saw the tears in her eyes but it wasn't enough.

"I have to Caro. I can't stay here with you and him across the hall. You can't expect me to...even a friend wouldn't be so cruel to expect that."

Caro gasped, her heart squeezed painfully and she couldn't answer him because he was right. He was absolutely right, she had hurt him, hurt them, and he didn't deserve any of it. She didn't know why it was happening to her or what it was about Noah but she couldn't ask Jon to wait it out with her...she couldn't hurt him anymore.

She ran out of his apartment to her own.

He shouldn't follow her, it was better to end it this way. He sighed deeply and followed her. He caught her before she closed the door and stepped into her apartment, slowly he drew her to him.

"Caro, I love you...I love you more than I ever should have," he touched her cheek softly, "but you know I can't be here while you're discovering your feelings for Noah. You understand that don't you?"

Caro nodded. She wouldn't hurt Jon anymore.

"I understand," she whispered.

"I'll be leaving for Connecticut tonight. I'll stay at the apartment above my parent's garage until I can sublet my apartment here."

He kissed her softly, and they both knew he was kissing her goodbye.

"You're really going tonight?" She knew she was losing him forever and her heart was breaking.

"I've finished all the strips through the holidays. I had a lot of time to work on them this weekend, I only have to drop them at the office and then I'll be free to leave...tonight," he turned from her and began walking to his apartment.

"Will you call me when you get there?" she whispered.

A short derisive laugh escaped him but he didn't turn to her for tears had formed in his eyes and he wouldn't let her see them. "No, I can't."

He quickly walked into the sanctuary of his own apartment where his heart could break in solitude and his pride would not be forfeit.

Caro leaned back against the cool wall and let the tears fall. A prayer formed in her heart and it was a prayer she felt throughout her entire being. It escaped from her and was heard on high and the council gathered at the sound and a decision was made.

Her prayer would be answered.

*   *   *

Noah was going for the gold tonight. He stood before the vanity mirror and viewed the dark suit critically. The perfect cut of it enhanced his appearance but he didn't see it. He saw only the worry in his eyes that she would deny him.

He pulled the velvet box from his pocket and looked at the flawless diamond. He had never wanted anything as much as her love. His hand shook as he placed the box back in his pocket and patted it. He snapped off the lights and left the house.

Tonight would define the rest of his life.

Caro couldn't stop thinking about Jon, the way he'd looked when he left. The pain her indecision had caused him...had caused all of them. And yet, here she sat in a posh restaurant at a candlelit table with Noah.

Admittedly, he also held a power over her.

"You're very quite tonight." Noah leaned across the table to take her hand in his and his breath fanned the flame of the candle.

"I'm sorry. It's just that Jon and I talked this afternoon and he...he decided it was best for him to go away while I'm seeing you."

199

Noah leaned back, unsure if her words boded well for him or not.

"Does that mean if you marry me he won't come back?" he tried for levity but the seriousness of the statement came through.

Caro looked up sharply. "Marry?" her palms began to sweat and her heart skipped a beat. The word always caused this reaction in her. Mitch had her running away scared all those years ago and now Noah had only mentioned it casually but the reaction was even worse, more worrisome with him.

"Why would you say that?" she laughed nervously hoping her fears were unfounded but when he began to reach for something in his pocket she feared they weren't.

"I was going to wait for the right moment and some moonlight but maybe it was meant to be now...I can't live without you Caroline. I know we haven't gone as far in our relationship for me to be dreaming of forever with you but I can't help it, I am. Forever is exactly what I want with you...I've known from the moment we met that I could love you... and...I do love you Caroline...very much." He slid the small black velvet box in front of her and waited for her cry of joy, it wasn't coming.

In the silence, Noah began to worry.

Stupidly, Caro stared at the box and wondered why they always put engagement rings in little black boxes, so solemn, so grave. It was a little black box that could seal her fate, close her in. She hated the look of it and she felt anger at Noah for being so presumptuous in their relationship and it felt good and right to be angry at him.

"Noah. I didn't expect this...I don't think I've decided how I even feel about us yet. I can't say if I love you."

"Can you say you don't?"

She looked up quickly. His eyes bore into hers intensely and Caro couldn't deny there was an attraction. "No, not definitively, but still--" she tried to explain her thoughts but Noah cut her off.

"What do you feel when you're with me Caro? Do you feel as if we've know each other...known each other very well?"

"There is something, but--"

Noah pressed his finger against her lips silencing her denial of love for him. He was convinced she was just afraid to admit it.

"Caro, listen to me," he murmured moving his fingers from her lips to her throat in a sensual caress, "even though we've never been intimate, I feel as if I know every inch of you, body and soul...Do you feel that too?" he traced the delicate curve of her neck and she shivered at his touch. He felt heartened by her reaction.

Caro couldn't deny the images his words invoked or the feelings his touch stirred. What he said was all true. She had intimate images of them that were impossible to explain.

"I do... but I don't understand *why* I feel this way. How can I logically feel this when I don't truly know you? I'm not happy about this strange recognition between us. It feels like I'm missing something...some piece to this puzzle between us. And it's a piece I need to find." She looked away. She was getting angry at herself and him...mostly at him.

Noah was frustrated at her refusal to accept what was between them. He had to try to make her see their future as he did, because he knew it would be a perfect match. He knew it and she did too, she was just not accepting it.

"Maybe it's because you fight against calling it what it is."

"What do you mean?" she looked back at him with curiosity.

"What you call recognition is really love. You just don't want to accept it." Noah leaned back in his chair feeling annoyed at her. He'd always thought that if you found love you were lucky, and you'd be crazy not to embrace it wholeheartedly. That was his parent's example to him and a lesson learned from their happy marriage. Noah wanted what they'd had and he felt he could have that and more with Caro. Why was she fighting it when he knew she felt it too?

"It's not that easy." She fumed at him folding her arms across her chest in anger.

"Why isn't it?" He demanded and his jaw tightened with annoyance.

*   *   *

The karmically fraught, romantic dinner played before Orion and he shook his head.

"They are going in circles. They'll never find the end to this. We must offer some insight to help them move on from here or I fear three souls will be tortured. This has to end."

David nodded, "I think we should give them a glimpse of themselves…their complete selves. It might be just what they need to force a decision."

Orion listened to David's plan and agreed.

David would be the one to intervene, since he had already connected with Caro once in her new life it would be logical for him to be the one to step in… and in the next few seconds all was set.

CHAPTER 21

"Caroline? Is that you?" the tall, dark, impressively handsome older man strolled up to their table.

"Hello, Professor McKay. I haven't seen you at the planetarium's discussion groups in quite a while. How have you been?" Caro latched on to any distraction to end the uncomfortable topic of love and marriage with Noah.

"I've been busy with other projects these last few weeks but today I had some business in this area of the city...It is so nice to run into you. How have you been?"

"I still love my job--"

The cough from Noah drew her attention and she realized she was being rude. She blushed and smiled weakly as she made the introductions.

"I'm so sorry, I thought you might have met at the Planetarium," Caro looked from one man to the other but Noah shook his head negatively as did Professor Mckay, "Professor David Mckay this is my good friend Noah Bradley. He's also an astrophysicist at the planetarium."

"I'm very pleased to meet you." David held out his hand to Noah who reluctantly stood up to grasp it.

"Same here," Noah replied. It was a firm grip and Noah found his masculine ego needed to grip back but in that handshake something transpired.

Noah let go and sat back down slowly, feeling unfocused and confused.

"I won't linger and disturb your meal Caro." Professor McKay placed his hand over hers as she smiled up at him.

"Are you sure you won't join us for a drink?" she asked hopefully, still wanting a diversion.

"No, I'm afraid I can't but thank you for the invitation. Enjoy your dinner Caro," he whispered and squeezed her hand slightly before letting go.

Caro nodded but she suddenly felt dizzy and as David smiled down at her she saw images forming around him. She had to lower her gaze from the brightness of those images.

When she lifted her eyes she refocused on Noah. Noah?

No, his name isn't Noah. Caro's heart pounded with the truth. His name was Dylan; and he was her husband.

In quick flashes it all came back to her, every day of their life together then and now and all the levels in between. Oh yes, they had a lot to discuss and apparently he knew it too, because he was staring back at her with recognition, he knew her too.

"Hi, Angel," he whispered shyly.

"Hi, yourself Dylan," she replied sharply.

Dylan shook his head," You're still angry at me?"

"Shouldn't I be? You left me Dylan. You didn't have to. I've wanted to yell at you for so long but I never had the chance. *You* never gave me the chance. So since that day…the day I went into labor…I've wanted to know, how could you leave me that way?"

"You actually think I had a choice?" Dylan was floored by that concept. Angelica had harbored a deep anger at him for dying? He never knew that. "Why would you think that I would choose to leave you?"

"Because when I was sent to guide others I realized how people make foolish decisions that affect the outcome of their lives and the lives of those who love them…you made a selfish decision that day and left me and our son alone."

"How did you ever come to that conclusion?" Dylan was baffled by her thinking; all he remembered of that fateful night was how much he wanted to reach her. How much he wanted to be with her in the ambulance, so she wouldn't be alone.

"Because with you it was always about being perfect, wasn't it Dylan?" she began softly, "Think about it, you could have stayed home with me that day. Remember how my pains had started the night before but you said you couldn't stay home with me. You're exact words as I remember were, 'Ah Angel, I want to be here but I have to finish that project, you know my boss is depending on me to bring it in on time. I don't want to let him down and first babies always take a little time. I'll be home before you know it.' That was what you'd said."

"I believed I would be-"

"Of course you did, you could never ruin your perfect record with your boss or in any other area of your life. You had to be everything to everyone. Funny thing is I would hunger for a little imperfection in you, a day of spontaneity. Just enough to show you cared about me more than some internal score card you needed to keep."

"Angel, believe me I never meant to leave you for that long. The client wanted changes at the last minute, I was just getting all the details when I got the call. You know I wanted to be with you. I didn't finish taking those notes I went rushing home to you-"

"And again...You didn't have to rush home Dylan. You could have driven calmly to the hospital...but no, you *had* to be the perfect husband accompanying his wife in the ambulance. If you'd taken the road to the hospital you would have arrived safely. The road to the hospital from your office wasn't through the mountain pass and it didn't ice up in a flash hail storm like the road home always did."

"You really don't understand...I wanted to get to *you*, just to you. I didn't care about some image I only thought of you in pain and needed to be there for you." Dylan tried to convince her but inside he felt a small spark of guilt begin. In a way, she was right. He was always thinking of what was the right thing to do and never straying from the straight course he'd set to achieving it, and it did cause tunnel vision in his reactions. He didn't always consider the other persons opinion. That day he hadn't considered hers.

"If only you could have been just a little imperfect that day, I would have loved you all the more for it Dylan. But even after that life ended, I wanted to see you...after living my life with out you and raising our son alone, I could have let this anger go if only..." she hesitated and shook her head.

"What?" he was afraid to ask but he needed to know.

"Dylan, you didn't even let me confront my feelings when I died, you purposely stayed away from me, leaving me to fester in my anger, struggling so much with it, I couldn't help others and the alternative was to be born again. Now I have all this karma-" she stopped as tears formed in her eyes.

"I'm sorry," he whispered.

"Why *did* you avoid me? And did you have anything to do with my not remembering our life when I was a guardian?"

"I didn't mean to…it wasn't …Yes, I did. I thought it was better for you to forget and go forward, but you're right, I couldn't face your anger. I felt it all the while you still lived, and I felt helpless when you died, but I thought you'd get over it. So yes,, I requested your training and hoped that after you'd seen every life has its pitfalls you'd learn that souls can be perfected and move on-"

"But Dylan…you didn't let me move on."

"I thought the training would-"

"No Dylan, The training only confused me more. If I'd been able to see you and confront my issues, you'd have had to admit to being less than perfect, but you couldn't face that. So instead, you tried to mold me again by trying to train me as a guardian when I wasn't ready to be one and now, in this new life, you had to step in and make me over…take me over again…" she hesitated and her eyes turned questioning. "Why *did you* come back?" She asked him curiously.

"I wanted a chance at a new life with you. I wanted to make it a better life for us…a better ending."

"You did?"

"I did."

"So were you part of this life plan when I was sent back or did you ask to be sent here after I met Jonathon?"

"What?"

"You heard me."

Dylan looked into her eyes knowing she deserved the truth.

"I asked to be a part of it…after."

"You should have let me have our past life memories and allowed me my anger over it and maybe, I would have become a guardian and maybe we'd have been good together but because you didn't allow me that, I had to take a new level of training…a new lifetime to work it all out and now I find…you couldn't let me do that either."

Dylan felt the truth in every word she hurled at him but he still felt what he did was built on love for her and he needed her to know that.

"I love you Angel. I always have. I've made mistakes. I'll admit that."

"It's too late Dylan. Don't you see I can't live up to the standards you've set for your life partner? I never could and this time wouldn't be any different. We aren't meant-"

Dylan stood up and pulled her from her chair. "Don't say it. Please don't. I don't want perfect anymore, I don't need to always be right. I realize I've missed a few steps in life myself, and now…I just want you, just you, as you are. No changes necessary because I love-."

Angelica put her hand over Dylan's lips to stop his words.

"No, I can't let you believe we can go on. These insights we've been given, seeing all we've been to each other, allowed me to see my true feelings and for the first time, I *know* myself…and I know my feelings are strong and sincere."

"Thank you. I'm so glad you-"

"No, you don't understand, Dylan you need to listen. I've formed a strong attachment to a rather imperfect man. One who loves me beyond reason; loves my quirks and insecurities as much as my strengths. I can finally accept his love and tell him I love him just as deeply. I could never say that to him because of all the pent up fears I was carrying around."

"No, you can't love him, you love me."

Their eyes locked as she whispered, "Dylan, you *have* to let me go."

"Angel, we're meant to be together," his eyes pleaded.

"No Dylan we aren't. We both need something beyond what we had. We can learn from this, I've wanted to tell you that for a long time but I never had the chance. I'm telling you now, we can both move forward."

Dylan shook his head refusing to hear her.

"No, please Angel, I'll be there for you. You loved me before and I know you can forgive me and love me again. We can make it end better this time. I love you," he pleaded fiercely.

"Dylan, I forgive you, I forgive us, but I'm not who you need and if you searched your heart honestly you'd find you don't really love me. Not the soul searing way you should. You just needed to set your perfect record straight but I can't give up another life helping someone I care about find theirs. This time, I have to find mine."

"Angel, I love you. Don't you remember the love between us…the passion?"

She took his hand in hers, "Our life, that life, ended Dylan and you have to let go of it too. I love Jon more than anything and it's unconditional, wacky, selfless,

209

funny, kind and wonderful and if he still loves me, I want to give him the rest of my days." She squeezed his hand wanting him to understand. She did love him but she was not in love with him.

Pain ripped through Dylan like nothing he'd ever felt before. Rejected and hurt, he knew he would have given all for her. In fact, thinking about it, he had given all for her. He'd reentered life and gambled that he could win her back. The prospect of this new life wasn't as bright as when he'd begged Orion to let him be reborn. Now he'd have to live all the days of this life without her. It didn't feel too rewarding knowing she would be living her days with Jonathan.

The crushing reality of her decision hit him hard but he had no choice left. She'd given him no choice…he'd let her go, he had to let her go and as he accepted it as truth, he had a revelation.

Orion had let him come here to do just that. The Wise Old Soul had known all along it was Dylan who needed to let go, not Angelica.

He smiled sadly and nodded to her, "I'll give you what you want, Angel. I'll let go of us and wish you well."

Dylan's hand released hers and immediately the room seemed to go out of focus for them both. They sat back down in their chairs and just as quickly the room refocused.

Caro felt a mild confusion. What had Noah just said? He'd asked her a question. He'd asked her about marriage.

Caro looked down at the black box in front of her and shivered. He'd asked her to marry him, but she knew she couldn't. She looked up at him and for the first time, she felt no confusion, no pull of attraction and no reason to deny what she felt.

210

No, she couldn't marry Noah and she knew why she couldn't, one very important reason why, and she needed to end this date and this relationship completely and hope it wasn't too late to stop Jon from leaving her.

Noah watched Caroline shake her head and knew her answer would not be the one he'd wanted, planned on, but he would hear it. He needed to hear it.

She slid the box across the table to him and said softly, "I'm so sorry Noah, I just don't love you. I know I've been unsure of how I felt but tonight, with this ring in front of me, it's all become clear. I haven't stopped thinking about Jon since this afternoon and I'm surer now then I've ever been that I'm in love with him."

Noah's green eyes shone with a sadness that went soul deep but he smiled at her with bravado.

"I can only accept your decision Caro and although I feel like the very pit of despair right now, I really do wish you all the happiness you can find," he placed the ring box back in his pocket.

"If we go now you might be able to catch him before he leaves," Noah said as he stood up and held his hand out to her.

Caro stared at it for half a heartbeat.

"You'd drive me back? Oh Noah! Thank you!" She jumped up from the table and kissed him.

He nearly pulled her closer for more but knew it was just a gesture and it was all he'd have to live on for the rest of his days.

He took her hand and tugged, "let's go."

CHAPTER 22

Jon was zipping up his suitcase when the pounding started on his door.

"Who the hell is that?" He grumbled sourly then turned and banged his knee into the open drawer of his nightstand and cursed ferociously. Whoever it was had better be in dire need of assistance or they soon would be, he thought darkly. He was in no mood for any company. Caro's decision to see Noah had hurt him deeply and it wouldn't take much to unleash his anger. He pulled open the door ready to brush off whoever dared to bother him and instantly his expression froze.

Caro launched herself into his arms, his arms closed around her.

Jon wasn't sure if he was having a wishful dream and really standing at the door hugging a deliveryman, or if his thoughts had brought her to him, but her soft voice slowly made him conscious of the reality of her.

"Oh Jon, forgive me...please forgive me, I love you, I always have. I was just so afraid to trust loving anyone...or that anyone could love me with all my imperfections. I was afraid to risk losing you. All foolish reasons, I know that now. Please believe I love you...only you," she hugged him tightly but he stood there unmoving.

Caro took his face in her hands and made him look at her, "Here's the strangest part, I don't know how, but tonight Noah helped me see it all clearly. How I was afraid to commit to love but then I realized I do love someone...I love him very, very much and I've loved him from the day I met him when I was five years old. I met my soul mate in kindergarten. It's you Jon...only you," she whispered softly and kissed his lips, his cheeks and every part of his face that she could reach standing on tiptoe.

Slowly, Jon registered her words. Her perfume filled his nostrils, her soft hair brushed his cheek, and her words became clearer, each one struck his heart, each one more poignant than the one before. Except for the name Noah, that one he refused to hear at all, each word was a balm to his pain, but still he held back. There was something more he needed from her.

He put his hands on her shoulders and moved her back so he could look into her eyes.

"Caro?" he whispered.

"Yes?"

She moved to kiss him again and, although it was hard to deny her, he held her firmly by the shoulders slightly away from his needy body. It was important she focus on his words..

"I need you to listen to me."

"Yes?"

"I don't want to go on living the way we have. I want us to marry, have kids, and tangle our laundry and our lives forever. Do you love me enough for that kind of commitment? Will you marry me?" he asked and waited for the denial, the double talk and the myriad of evasive reasons that always came from Caro with this topic but instead, a smile so brilliantly angelic appeared on her face nearly blinding him.

"Yes! Oh Heavens yes! I will marry you and love you enough to commit to that and then some!" she launched herself into his arms.

"Yes?" Jon repeated bewildered, "You said yes?" he pulled her back again to look at her, her smile beamed happily up at him. Was he going crazy? This was his Caro, the Caro that avoided commitment to the bitter end. Had she just said yes to him?

"Yes, Jon I will marry you!" Caro said forcefully and waited for it to sink in.

It didn't take long.

She was crushed in his arms an instant later, and loving him a moment beyond that.

*   *   *

Later that night, Jon grilled steaks on the terrace and after dinner he poured them wine and brought her a dessert. On a silver tray sat a strange looking fortune cookie. It appeared to be made of gold.

That can't be too edible, she thought as she picked it up and indeed she found it was solid metal.

214

"Read your fortune." Jon prompted her softly.

Caro turned the cookie over in her hand and pulled at the white silk strip of paper that hung from the side. Its message caused her no fear, only immense joy. It read simply, 'marry me.'

She smiled up at him. "I already said I would."

She reached out to him but he shook his head.

"It isn't official yet. Open the cookie."

"Open it? How?" she looked at the solid cookie and noticed a small line that seemed to go around the center. She tried to break it but then she twisted the cookie and it snapped open. A beautiful ruby and diamond ring fell out.

Caro stared at the ring not believing how alive she felt by this gift.

It was perfect, no little black box, no cold white diamond. Instead a ring that sparkled with bright fiery life winked up at her, surrounded by the warm gold of the odd ring box.

"When did you decide to marry me?"

"Caro I've had that ring in that drawer since we started really dating and until tonight I thought it would stay there forever."

"Oh Jon, you're so perfect for me." She started to cry as she confessed, "I love you. I always have. I'm sorry I couldn't tell you sooner."

He pulled her up to him and whispered, "So will you marry me?"

She laughed, "Yes, I'll marry you."

The kiss sizzled like the brilliance of the gems in her new ring.

Jon lifted her up and into his arms as he confessed, "I'm not perfect Caro but you already know all my imperfections and one idiosyncrasy that I've had since I met you. I loved you then, now and I'll love you always and forever."

"Oh Jon, we're both perfectly imperfect and forever is exactly how long I will love you."

Their kiss was filled with that promise of forever…and forever stretched before them for the taking.

*   *   *

(Council on High)

"I think that went very well don't you?" David turned to Orion and smiled widely.

"Yes…for Caroline and Jonathon but it will be a long two years for Noah before he's ready to accept love with Genevieve." Orion answered sagely.

"Genevieve?"

"Yes…their paths will cross in a couple of life months but Noah will be nursing his loss of Caroline for some time yet. It will take a bit of doing for Genevieve to get through to him but I think ultimately she will…and if my calculations are correct and baring their free will to give up…They should be married within three years and raising a family by four."

"So we shall have Noah back here by the end of this life span pursuing his attainment again?" David concluded but Orion shook his head prompting David to reassess his conclusion. "No? Why ever not, he was so close to it?" David asked curiously.

"Noah is going to like being in love for the first time, the real all consuming love that Genevieve will bring him. I think it will be quite awhile before he contemplates their existence out of the physical life. They may get it right the first time around or they may require a few more lifetimes to bring it to perfection. You see David, Genevieve is Noah's true soul mate. He'd derailed finding that relationship when he refused to go back to a rebirth after his life with Angelica had

216

ended so badly. He couldn't get past what he deemed was his failure with her and he was punishing himself by staying here and trying to avoid his own karma.

"So you knew all along that you were leading him back to the path of his destiny when he begged you to be reborn?"

"Lets say, tonight, for the first time he will let the pain from his past life dissipate and be free to move on and grow as he should have."

"So this was the plan for him?"

"This was the hope for him. You know as well as I David, wisdom and pureness are very necessary for attainment but to reach the highest attainment these gifts, as all things, must be tempered with love, true love. Love is the birth of everything and free will is always present."

David nodded and guessed.

"So we shall see Noah and Genevieve after two lifetimes together?"

"Two possibly three, of course the decision will be theirs."

"What of Caroline and Jonathon?"

"They will enjoy this life to the maximum of love's happiness, producing a large family and living a long life together."

Orion looked across time and saw the wedding of Caro to Jonathon at the moment their vows were spoken a rainbow appeared over their heads. They've found the *perfect path* together.

"Blessed be." Orion whispered before letting the image fade, after all he had much more to oversee but as for these three souls, all things considered, they were moving along splendidly.

Printed in Great Britain
by Amazon

39505007R00132